KU-778-129

About the Author

Garbhan Downey has worked as a journalist, broadcaster, newspaper editor and literary editor. He lives in Derry with his wife Una and children Fiachra and Bronagh. His previous publications include:

Running Mates (2007)
Off Broadway (2005)
Private Diary of a Suspended MLA (2004)
Creggan: More Than A History (2001),
co-author Michael McGuinness
Just One Big Party (1994)

This book is a work of fiction. All characters in this publication – other than those clearly in the public domain – are fictitious, and any resemblance to real persons, living or dead, is purely co-incidental. Due to the satirical nature of this book, some licence has been taken to include public figures in a number of fictitious scenes. We trust they will accept and enjoy their involuntary cameo roles in the spirit in which they were intended.

Acknowledgements

Many thanks for their time, expertise and encouragement to: Paul Hippsley, Declan Carlin, Kevin Hippsley, Jenni Doherty, and Aaron Murray of Guildhall Press; BAFTA-nominated animator John McCloskey for the cover; my father Gerry Downey for the vital first edit; and my eternally-supportive wife Una, without whom this book would have remained as scribbles in a jotter.

A special mention also to all at the Arts Council of Northern Ireland for their continuing assistance and to the Nerve Centre for letting us borrow John McC.

Finally, can I just bid a fond farewell to Bookworm bookshop in Derry – home not only to a couple of great launches, but also to hundreds of happy childhood memories.

On Politics

"It is double pleasure to deceive the deceiver."
Niccolo Machiavelli, author of The Prince.

"Never talk when you can nod, and never nod when you can wink, and never write an e-mail because it's death."
Eliot Spitzer, defrocked NY governor.

"Never forget, there is always someone smarter than you in the game."
Victor 'Switchblade Vic' McLaughlin,
retired North Derry paramilitary boss.

For Aine and Cecelia,
two wonderful grandmothers

PROLOGUE

For almost twenty years I've been telling him: if you want to get ahead in life, public or private, never put anything down on paper. The spoken word may occasionally catch up with you, but the written word will hang you ten times out of ten. Cardinal Richelieu, the age-old role model for twisted-bastard jurists like myself, used to say that if he had six lines written by even the most honest man, he could find enough therein to hang him. And Shay Gallagher, the Assembly Member for North Derry, despite what you may have been told, is not the most honest of men. After all, he is a politician – and quite a successful one.

Why Shay started committing his thoughts to pen and ink, I'm not sure. He himself claimed it was probably less dangerous than writing or speaking into any electronic device. He was hitting his mid-thirties, and like so many of us who grew up in the IT age, he was beginning to develop the same distrust of computers that older generations have of banks. And given that about half my client base are currently being prosecuted for computer-related crime, who am I to argue?

As his agent, I was happy enough to indulge Shay in this new departure – just as long as he made full daily use of the new Disintegrate 2000 Super-Shredder I installed in his Dunavady constituency office. This particular machine, according to experts, will turn a congressional library into a winter snowstorm before the Fraud Squad break through the first deadbolt.

So, you can gather that I was as astounded as anyone when I discovered that Shay had insisted on preserving the bulk of his correspondence – both incoming and outgoing alike – in an archive. A permanent, hard-copy archive, that is, which any half-baked burglar could lift right out of his strongbox when he wasn't around, without even having to go to the bother of cracking his PC password.

You'd think he'd have learned, after the near fiasco that was his five-year diary. But Shay was a teacher in his previous life and, as you'll remember, this is a species that knows everything there is to know already.

Shay, surprisingly, has always been a bit of a naïf when it comes to the potential malevolence of others. He could never see the harm in hanging onto, for example, his love letters to his fiancée, Sue McEwan, or his memos to his PA, Brendy, or his regular apology notes to Monsignor Giddens, his interfering confessor and former boss. He could never see how they could possibly be used against him, the poor innocent bastard. But, thankfully, he was generally savvy enough to abide by my '90 Per Cent Rule', which is this: there is no harm, occasionally, in planting a little white lie in a story – i.e. a 10 per center – if it can help you undermine the other 90 per cent or, alternatively, give it legs, at a later stage.

The 90 Per Cent Rule came in particularly handy in the latter part of the recent war here when the right to silence was abolished for paramilitary suspects. The change in the law meant that unless you answered their questions, the courts could safely assume that you had indeed gone around whacking everyone and blowing up everything just as they said you did. So as a way around this, our clients began making free admissions – most of which were true. But they always included one iron-clad lie which they knew they could disprove at a later date. And many a 'confession' was ruled invalid because, while our man certainly committed offences A through to I, he couldn't have done J, which he'd also coughed to, because he was out of the country at the time. But as soon as J is disproved before the court, the whole stack of cards collapses, as the admissions were obviously made under duress.

Apprised of this caveat, you, the reader, are now in a position to make your own mind up about Shay's role in this somewhat seedy account of murder, extortion and betrayal. He was careless to keep this record, no doubt, and he writes carelessly on many matters which smarter men would keep silent about. And to be honest, even when he does lie, he doesn't do it particularly well. No matter how hard you drill your protégés, they can always find new ways to fuck things up. But given that most of those directly involved in this particular tale are now dead, in jail, or otherwise beyond suing me, I suppose we can chance our arms and publish the damned thing.

But remember: nothing you read here is the complete truth, because, as our friend Jack Nicholson likes to remind us, 'You can't handle the truth . . .'

Tommy 'Bowtie' McGinlay BCL
(Constituency Manager and Editorial Advisor to Shay Gallagher MLA)

SEPTEMBER

Brainse Bhaile Thormod
Ballyfermot Library   Tel. 6269324/5

11

From: the Office of Shay Gallagher MLA
Stormont

To: Susan McEwan
Independent Unionist Assemblywoman
Carsonville, Greencastle, County Tyrone

Dear Sue

You're right, of course. The era of safe email is over. Pen and ink is much more secure. One of the wee Shinner soldier-ants told me that MI5 can read every single word typed into any computer here at Stormont. I asked him was that before or after the Provos had their turn? Earned me a long hard glare of republican disapproval: 'Tsk, and to think, Gallagher, you could have been one of us if only you'd had the cojones . . .'

I just hope none of them ever get their hands on the photo-attachment I sent to you of the pair of us the night of the great Assembly re-opening. And I agree entirely, videophone images will remain off-limits as well – or at the very least be restricted as to such times that we're stone-cold sober, fully dressed, and not in the Ladies' toilets of the Waterfront Hilton.

Having *says* all that (as our new Deputy First Minister is wont to remark), the act of committing words to paper can be equally dangerous. And I'm pretty damn sure my man Brendy will have a good read of this before he hands it on to your PA Lindsay who will also steam it open and reseal it before passing it on to you. But at least the pair of them are in our corner most of the time. It's not as if somebody is texting us up blind, asking us do we want a sports massage at the Ramada . . .

Anyhow, while you've been down in the sticks organising your new constituency office, I've been spending the last couple of days getting to know a few of the other faces up here at Parliament Buildings. Not that I've been speaking to them, mind. Christ knows you should never encourage them – some of them truly believe they're here to govern! Next thing, they'll be asking you to vote for their hare-brained bills. And as my old granny, God rest her, would say, if the Lord had meant you to take a stand, Shay, he would never have given you such a fine arse.

Leabharlanna Poibli Chathair Bhaile Átha Cliath
Dublin City Public Libraries

No, rather than indulging in face-to-face research, I've been fingering feverishly on my laptop and checking our new neighbours out on the Assembly website.

And let me immediately put your mind at rest: I've carefully perused the photo-gallery, and our titles of the Assembly's Number One Hunk and Honey are under no threat whatsoever.

Indeed, while I often heard it said that politics is a beauty contest for ugly people, I never thought that so many people would actually set out to prove it true. (I'm exempting, naturally, the deliciously truculent Iris – who still heads up my list of five 'alternates' – and Gerry Kelly, who would certainly top yours, if you could only forgive him for being a rebel.)

There are some particularly unfortunate photos. Sammy Wilson has forgone a tie in favour of a black Aran jumper which, and let's call a spade a spade here, almost makes him look like a Fenian. As for Mickey Brady, well, suffice to say, it is not for nothing that he is now known in these parts as An American Werewolf in Newry and Armagh. Then, capping them all, you have a sheet-white, terror-struck John O'Dowd, who clearly has just seen a ghost – or been asked to give evidence to the PSNI's Unsolved Crimes Squad.

Most of the members don't have their bios filled in – and those who do have roundly resisted the temptation to be in any way interesting. I decided to compile a list of ten MLAs I least want to get cornered in the canteen by, but wore myself out before I even got to Mark Durkan. One poor soul, in his list of hobbies, boasts of sitting on 447 separate committees, all of which have the words regional or development somewhere in the title. If ever a man were in a need of a weekend in Donegal with your good self, a four-pack of Powers and a set of furry handcuffs, it is he. Though, in saying that, I will give you £1,000 if you promise to warn me if he's ever within fifty feet of me at a party.

I'll finish now as it's almost lunchtime and there's a danger that some God-botherer will rattle on my door and ask me to break bread with them. Much rather be having a swift one with you – and a drink, if we've time.

Love always
Shay

Dearest Shay

I've never been really comfortable writing things down – and particularly not since Tommy Bowtie intercepted those rather, ah, intemperate emails we sent one another in the first heady days of our engagement. Lord, I still blush when I remember how I hit the Send To All button, instead of the Reply key. I sat screaming 'stop, stop, stop, you fucker' at it for a full thirty seconds before switching the computer off at the mains. Luckily, Tommy was the only other Contact on my home email – or the entire Agriculture Committee could have been reading in graphic detail how I intended to thank you for each and every carat in my 24-carat ring. And by the way, I've rethought Number 17. You can buy me all the jewellery you want and indeed the gin – but I'm not going there again. You can have an extra 21 on Sunday morning to make up. (Or maybe three 7s!)

I think you're right about pen and ink, though; it is safer. And in this age of semi-literate email and fully illiterate txt messages, hand-written letters have a real personal charm. Particularly now you've got that new shredder. Just don't make the same mistake one of the DUP MLAs did when he got his installed. He didn't realise it was one of those top-of-the-range jobbies that they make now for shredding CDs and nearly got pulled through the blades when his tie got caught in the teeth. Typical Antrim man, however – even as he was being sucked into the machine, he had the presence of mind to remove the wallet from his jacket pocket and throw it to the furthest corner of the room.

I've been spending most of my time here in the constituency office dealing with queries about the upgrading of the Dublin–Derry road. The new highway will inevitably lead to some of the smaller towns and villages being bypassed. So, as my old dad used to say, compensation is setting in. Chief among the plaintiffs is the Carnbally shopkeeper Leonard Kerins, a mean old sod, who, it's rumoured, still refuses to sweep out his floor or wipe down his ham slicer in protest at the Good Friday

Agreement. He reckons his passing trade will be halved. So, too, will salmonella and tapeworm in Mid-Tyrone. Though I was careful not to say that to him, as Lenny the Leech is also bigot-in-chief at the Carnbally Orange Lodge – and worth an easy eighty votes on polling day.

Most here, however, reckon the new road is a good thing. Parents of young children can stop living in fear of motorists flying through their towns. Jack Gilmore the cop says speeding is so prevalent that they only book drivers who are doing more than 15 mph ABOVE the limit. And yes, I know that's rich coming from a speed queen like myself – but at least I don't have six points on my licence like some I could mention. Two more tickets anytime over the next eighteen months and you'll be forced to get a lift up in the morning with the Shinners. And you just know they'll be reporting back your every word – just as surely as the Special Branch bug in the roof is.

I can understand you being tempted to join up with them – especially now they're dangling that committee chairmanship at you. A twenty-grand raise would buy a lot of pint bottles. But the thing I love most about you, my darling, is that you've always been your own man and can think for yourself. You don't have to leave the phone off the hook every time there's a bank robbery or punishment battering in darkest Dunavady. And you've never had to wait for the mantra to be wired down from Belfast before you stand in front of a live mike. You know your own mind.

It's the same reason I never signed up with the DUP. Whenever my Maker calls me home, I want to be able to tell Him I always tried to love each man and woman as myself: Catholic, Protestant, Black, White, Arab and Jew, homosexual, heterosexual, or downright pervert. (I will, however, make an exception for Manchester United fans and Free Presbyterians.)

The problem with independents like us is that we have little weight. As my mother is forever reminding me, if my politics wore my trousers, my arse would never look big. You and I are two lone voices among 110 on the Hill; so our best hope is always to grab the high moral ground of the Honest Broker and damn the rest of them for their grubby deal-making.

I'll close now, as I want to get out of the office before the Socialist Workers arrive to lobby me on the water rates. They made the appointment under a dummy name – but Lindsay on the front desk recognised a distinct staccato voice when they rang to confirm. And I've just had the place vacuumed.

See you on Friday night for a quick bite – and maybe a lamb pasanda afterwards.

Love always
Sue

Constituency Office of Shay Gallagher MLA
Main Street
Dunavady

Dear Sue

I'm still a little misty round the extremities from dinner last night and won't be meeting any clients until the Nurofen and breath mints do their job. You of all people should know by now you don't have to get me pie-eyed to wantonly disrespect you. But many thanks, regardless.

Brendy is out minding the front office, re-scheduling my 10.00 and 10.30, with assurances that the Assemblyman is in an urgent videoconference with a Stormont committee. He's a good kid, even if he hasn't got the brains to boil a kettle. Twice I've caught him in the past week fielding calls about what he is convinced is going to be my 'surprise' party. Both times he started babbling something about Mr Gallagher being more than happy to attend the 'thirty-fifth anniversary of Drumbridge Farmers' Co-operative', and yes, he'd see personally that the guest of honour would be in his seat in time. Clearly, Brendy is of the opinion that I was dropped on my head as a baby as well.

The thought of being thirty-five isn't so bad, as you'll discover in a few years time; well, not so long as you've the body of a twenty-six-year-old god (or, in your case, twenty-one-year-old goddess). The party is Tommy Bowtie's idea, of course. Psychological sleight of hand – make me wake up to the idea that all of a sudden I'm nearer forty than I am thirty so I'll rush off and marry you. Which I will, by the way, just as soon as you give the nod. I know you'd prefer to wait until the summer recess and hop off to Italy and do it all privately. But nine months is a long time – in life as in politics. And the new house will be ready by February. It's a shame to leave it empty so long. (You know you could always just hoist that pretty middle finger of yours to the God-fearing backbenches and come and live in sin with me until July.)

You were mentioning the new road is a big talking point down in Tyrone. In Dunavady, virtually everyone in the town is united against the proposed new bypass – Catholic, Protestant and East European dissenter alike. The traffic here isn't too problematic – and there are rarely any tailbacks, which means we don't tend to slow up commuters unduly. But the Chamber of Commerce predict the proposed route will lose us £5 million in passing trade a year. And more worryingly again, it takes us off the map when it comes to new industrial initiatives.

There's a multinational pharmaceutical company who make stomach powders – Dunsuffrin, they're called – who were really taken by the charms of the borough when they visited here last year. Of course, we sold them the virtues of the pure mountain water, the clean unpolluted air and our moderately well-educated (though not so clever you have to keep an eye on them) workforce. The locale here, we even suggested, would be picture perfect for filming their ads: peaceful forests, serene glens, gently lapping streams and comely maidens dancing to fiddles outside bars. (We can play the game, too, when we have to.)

So we got a tentative agreement that if Dunsuffrin ever came to the North, they'd make their base here. But this damn bypass reduces us to hick small-town status and there's already a rumour abroad that the company have been chatting to a few Derry gobshites, who of course have whinged so hard about never getting nothing that the Belfast gentry feel obliged to spot them a few jobs. And that's 200 salaries we could really do with here.

The real kicker in all of this, though, is our independent nationalist MP, Frank Bennett – or 'Bent' as he's more accurately referred to in these parts. Not only is he putting a 10 per cent bite on every Dunavady farmer lucky enough to have their land vested for the new road, but on top of that, he's getting a flat £1 million from the contractor appointed to complete the North Derry stretch of the project. And by 'appointed', I do of course mean 'hand-picked'.

Bent, it's alleged, could make himself £2 million clear by the time the last sod is turned. (Though with the grace of God, maybe someone will park him under it.) Tommy Bowtie is looking at ways to slow him up as we speak.

Talking of roads, I very much enjoyed your lecture about my speeding. The nerve of you – you're like a born-again Shinner giving sermons about fireworks. 'Don't do them, kids, they'll burn your fingers.' Three times have I sat in your car while you flirted your way out of penalty points. Three times! I was done for 41 in a 30 zone – you got off after driving 87 in a 60. There really are separate laws for redheaded, green-eyed babes. Oh, for more gay cops! I'd never get another ticket, I'll tell you.

Anyway, the fog is starting to lift a bit, so I'll go and make a start on the day.

I love you more than ever
Shay

Carsonville
Greencastle

My dearest Shay

Rest assured, I'll go easier on the brandy-pouring tomorrow night. Jesus, drinking on a Tuesday is a definite no-no. It's all right for you; you can survive on a couple of hours sleep – but if I don't get my eight hours, I'm as crabbed as a DUP picket line. And by the way, I know I don't have to feed you drink to make you love me – though in case you haven't noticed, it does just slow you up a little . . .

I'm sorry that living together isn't an option. Really. I suppose it's why we tend to overdo it on our midweek hook-ups. But truth is, I need the church groups to keep the seat. And bad enough

I'm going to be shacked up with a hell-bound Fenian, but they'd drop me quicker than a ticking box if we were to move in together before I got my wedding band.

Like yourself, I'd get married in the morning, but it's going to take to early summer till we get Danielle's adoption papers processed. She's thrilled you're going to be her daddy; well, as thrilled as any cynical fourteen-year-old is ever likely to get. Keeping her was the best thing I ever did – jointly with agreeing to be your wife, she added rapidly (and unnecessarily).

I think you may have to kiss goodbye to the Dunsuffrin plant – we had to, in Mid-Tyrone. Ultimately, they won't hack the thought of paying ten cents in the dollar more tax up here than they would south of the border (thanks to our ridiculously high rates for corporations) – unless of course we bribe them. You, being you, had the advantage of a guaranteed start-up grant you shook out of Dublin in return for your support in other matters. But now that Derry have their claws into them and are evens-favourite to get the seed money you thought you'd locked up, I fear the jobs are gone.

Derry have a purpose-built plant ready and a hundred high-tech staff just waiting at the end of a phone. Big money is like big women: they like to reproduce as quickly as possible. And big money always goes for the safest option – which is why it stays big money.

I agree that Frank Bent is doing you no favours with the new road. But he goes back so long and knows where so many corpses are hidden that you're never going to catch him with his fingers in the box. The only consolation with people like him is that they always end up running into someone dirtier than themselves. (Though in fairness to Frank, he'll probably have to die first.)

Your best bet for stalling the bypass is to demand public hearings first. Get the thing into a courtroom and Tommy Bowtie can delay construction work for a year at least. Raise some environmental issue – rare squirrels are good, or maybe a unique form of plant life. We stopped an incinerator outside Teacherstown last year by showing the High Court film footage of Ulster's last remaining silver shrew colony. God bless Google and a man who knows how to Photoshop from Russian internet sites. There hasn't been a silver shrew in Ireland since Bairbre de Brún got that last dye job. (Mi-aow! Apologies. I know, those days are over.)

Seriously, though, your worst problem seems to be that Bent doesn't give a damn about his seat, because he's retiring at the next Westminster election. He has his fortune made, and if he ever needs pin money, he can always blackmail himself onto a few quangos.

You should really be thinking about that seat, by the way. Maybe that's why you don't want to upset the incumbent, you sly dog? The Shinners don't have the numbers – nor do the Stoops. Much better an agreed nationalist than risking a split vote and letting in some square-headed Proddy. Fianna Fáil would probably even fund your campaign on the qt. It would do no harm at all to their recruitment drive in the North – just as long as it could never be said they were recognising another parliament in their own country . . . Hmm. 'Mrs Shay Gallagher, Member of Parliament.' Now, that has a ring to it.

By the way, I know nothing about any surprise birthday party for you. But coincidentally, myself and Danielle have been invited to the top table of the Drumbridge Farmers' Co-operative thirty-fifth anniversary dinner next week. And I have been instructed to make the keynote speech, despite the fact I wouldn't know a Drumbridge farmer if he bit my arse through a thorny hedge. Please remember to act surprised, if only for Brendy's sake. He's been working on this so long we've all started calling him Stakeknife.

I've a full office outside, so I'll close this now, replete as ever with all my love. It'll not be long until we're together forever, my darling. And until then, sure we can continue enjoying our regular, ah, stopovers.

Love always
Sue

Members' Offices
Stormont

Dear Sue

The MP's job would be tempting all right, if only to lord it over the various flocks of sheep who managed to get themselves elected to the chamber up here. It really puts hair in my soup that they think they've got the inside track because they can all sing the same words to a few dismal hymns.

But the dirty little secret, as you and I both know, is that not only do backbench MLAs have no influence, neither do their bosses. And no matter how pretty London and Dublin tell us we're looking, or what a wonderful job we are doing of running their bastard state, we are no more a government than the board of directors of Dunavady Town FC.

We administer a small budget, 90 per cent of which is already pre-spent on schools and hospitals. We have no fund-raising powers ourselves, other than the begging bowl and rates increases; the first of which is becoming less effective now we've stopped shooting people, and the second, of course, will get us de-selected.

We are a million people fewer than Manchester – yet our security budget is about a hundred times higher. And, as you pointed out, our tax on businesses is 10 per cent higher than our nearest neighbour. If all that's not bad enough, two out of every three jobs here are funded by the British Exchequer. Our livelihood is entirely dependent on Downing Street.

At least if a man is in the House of Commons, he's playing in a grown-up game. There's always the chance there that you can twist an arm or call in a favour and get your patch a new factory – as Hume used to.

Mark my words, the day that the Shinners find themselves in a position to swing a Westminster vote, they'll take their seats to an Orange band playing. It's all about putting the swill in the trough. The Romans had it right – politics boils down to two things: bread and circuses. Keep the public fed and keep them distracted, and they'll not bother you. Or as it is today, Big Macs and Big Brother.

Why not pitch for the Dáil, you might ask. Fianna Fáil's plans to set up in the North could open doors for a handsome young JFK in the making. (Without the unfortunate ending – and, of course, the women.) But, as generations of Northern nationalists are aware, the South have a hundred years' experience of leading us to the altar and leaving us there. As soon as they see the priest, they're running away quicker than

Julia Roberts when she worked out about Richard Gere what the rest of us suspected all along.

Ultimately, it doesn't really matter if the parliament is British or Irish these days, as we all do what we're told by the Americans anyway. For the minute, though, I'll probably have to content myself with the Dunavady mayoralty next year. It's my turn under the D'Hondt system, and while the job entails little more than cutting ribbons and eating dodgy shrimp, it'll heighten my profile a bit for whenever the glorious day comes. And besides, if I don't take the post, it could fall to that awful anti-everything bigot Fulcroom Lydock.

The bypass issue here is hotting up – I've got to dash now and write to a couple of farmers who're (rightly) convinced that Bent is screwing them over the land sales. One got roasted for refusing to sell; the other's just found out he only got half of what everybody else did for his tract. How Bent managed to snatch 50 per cent of a vested sale – on top of his regular 10 per cent kickback – is beyond me. I'm not sure whether to loathe him or admire his rampant amorality.

Looking forward to seeing you tonight for our tête-à-tête. (At least to begin with.)

Love always
Shay

To: Paul Parks
Hillcrest Farm
Caslanvady

Dear Mr Parks

Frank Bennett is indeed, as you so neatly put it, a 'cute fucker of the highest order'. And that statement I write confidently here as a public representative, knowing that no court in the land will consider it libellous.

Mr Bennett, however, is such a cute fucker that his fingerprints are nowhere near this deal. There is no evidence he creamed off the other £150,000 from the land deal as you have alleged (and everybody with half a brain knows to be true). Unfortunately, you signed the damned contract yourself – happy with what you were getting for what, let's face it, is twelve acres of mountain bog you couldn't rear sheep on.

I am truly sorry your farming colleagues think that you are a horse's windhole for not conferring with them about the price. But you, you clever man, managed to get a cheque into your hand from Mr Bennett directly – such as none of your neighbours have yet seen. And you will be delighted to hear that there is to be a challenge to the bypass route announced this week, which is going to set Pangur Bán among the pigeons. You might just be the luckiest fellow in the borough after all.

Yours
Shay Gallagher BA (Hons) DipEd
Member of the Legislative Assembly for North Derry

PS Thanks for your support, as always, on polling day, Paul.

To: Daniel Broderick
Ardnashee Farm
Caslanvady

Dear Mr Broderick

I agree entirely that putting Frank Bennett in charge of the bypass was like putting Al Capone in charge of the Credit Union.

Likewise, I have no doubt that he deliberately stopped the purchasing of your land because you refused him his cut. And, as you say, it is 'plain bastarding ludicrous' that the new road has to be extended by two miles to veer around your farm.

You will, thus, be relieved to learn that all vesting orders concerning the bypass are likely to be revoked within the next month or so. Thomas McGinlay, my constituency manager, is to seek an injunction next week, delaying the project for a minimum of one year – so that Mr Bennett and his development company associates can meet the terms of the consultation process, which was promised but never delivered.

Yours
Shay Gallagher BA (Hons) DipEd
Member of the Legislative Assembly for North Derry

PS We're guaranteed getting the order, Danny, so don't panic. Bent has ticked off so many high court judges in his time, he'll probably not even set foot in the court to defend it.

Carsonville
Greencastle

Dearest Shay

Sure enough, the old bat began giving me a hard time as soon as I came through the door last night. You Fenians think your mothers have a monopoly on guilt – well, let me tell you, us Smoked Cods know a thing or two about mental torture as well.

It's really no-win. If you come down here for the weekend, it's separate rooms and herself sleeping with both ears open. But if I go up to Dunavady without Dani, I'm an unfit mother. And if I bring her with me, I'm a tramp setting a bad example. As if! I'm thirty-two years old and the only man I've ever been with while fully conscious, not vomiting and not on my Freshers' night is you. Mum knows I'm uptight, but, and plays on it.

I know it's expensive, but weekends away are our best bet – at least that way the three of us can pretend we each have our own rooms. Though in saying that, both Danielle and myself will need a bunk at your casa on Friday coming, as the 'Co-op anniversary' is likely to run on into the wee hours. And no, you can't run away. Brendy would have a little gay breakdown. (I don't care what I promised you on Saturday night. You were, ah, badgering the witness at the time.)

Frank Bent's going to be there, by the way, if only to stop us ripping the back off him, as is at least one Stormont minister. So you'll have to shave. Hope whoever the Executive send down is a drinker so we can let our hair down a bit – though the odds are horribly against us. Say what you want about the Stoops and the Ooops, but at least they occasionally remove the sticks from their arses.

I see from this morning's *News Letter* that Bent is livid about the upcoming challenge to the bypass. But knowing our man, I would be pretty certain he got most of his finder's fees up front. And the chances of anyone getting a cent back out of him are slim. I just hope for his own sake he didn't put the arm on the wrong guy. You did well not to attach your name to the challenge – though with Tommy Bowtie handling it, everyone knows it's got your imprimatur.

Word is that the Loyalist Action Group – or whatever they call themselves now they've scrubbed off their ACAB* tattoos – were very annoyed that Bent had studiously avoided dealing with them over the road. One of their main men in your parts, Victor McLaughlin (known in his police file for a whole lot of less-than-salubrious reasons as Switchblade Vic), owns most of the land on what could have been an alternative Dunavady bypass route. Indeed, if Tommy's challenge succeeds, you could end up making Vic a very, very rich man. How's that for cross-community co-operation! One of my dodgy loyalist friends informed me that Vic was so annoyed at Bent's proposed route that he was considering gifting the MP his own little portion of mountain bogland, free gratis. But he was overruled on the grounds that we all love one another again (at least as long as the cheques keep coming in). Curiously, Vic and Bent had regularly done business together up until pretty recently – thus confirming what we knew all along about thieves and honour.

Talking of dodgy loyalists, I agree with you on one level that withholding cash from these groups', ahem, 'community projects', is as good a way as any to limit their bad behaviour. But what happens when our well of little bribes dries up?

---

* Twentieth-century acronym questioning the validity of Roman Catholic marriage certificates.

My accountant tells me that the third biggest industry in the world, after oil and finance, is . . . ? You got it – crime. Do you really suppose that we can construct a crime-free society out of what was here before? Maybe it's my late, unlamented father's judicial genes coming out in me at last, but until every group whose acronym begins with a U, R or I hands in its hardware, I don't think we've a chance.

At the risk of appearing self-righteous, I'm starting to feel sorry for those among us who have never resorted to physical-force blackmail – particularly all the good little children in the UUP and SDLP. But as you're well aware from your last career as a teacher, Shay, you can never control a classroom until you sort out the rowdies at the back first.

If all this sounds grumpy, blame my mother – and the post-weekend hangover. God, that Hennessy XO is easy drunk. Just a pity we used up all the cream before we thought of making Alexanders. Maybe we'll get in a fresh tin for Wednesday night at the Hilton!

Love always
Sue

To: The Eyrie
Ardshane
Dunavady

Dear Mr Gallagher

I am posting this letter to your home, as I have to make sure it does not fall into the hands of the 'man' who handles the mail at your office.

Your PA, Brendan Gallagher, who I believe is actually a second cousin of yours, was sighted in a notorious Derry nightclub at the weekend, drinking blackcurrant alcopops and dancing with a well-known homosexual in tight trousers. They left the club together, giggling like schoolgirls, and were then seen going into an apartment on the quay. There, I can only assume, some highly improper conduct – totally unbecoming of a public representative's representative – took place. Though I have, as yet, no conclusive evidence of this, as our sergeant wouldn't let us raid the flat.

Nonetheless, I will keep tabs on the situation for you, and as soon as I have prima facie proof of your assistant's unseemliness, I will forward it directly to you.

Yours in confidence
'Serpico'

Memo: SG/TB

Hi, Tommy

I think we should find out who this Serpico guy is, quietly and as soon as possible. He seems like a most interesting character. (See attached.)

Shay

———————

Like Shay, I have to say I was immediately intrigued by Serpico's letter. Nutters tend to latch onto politicians. They realise that, despite their madness, they still possess something that each and every elected representative holds most dear – i.e. a vote. But Serpico was no ordinary psycho – he was controlled, reasoned and was clearly after something more than just young Brendy's scalp. Serp, whoever he was, had ambition. He was also demonstrating to us that he had access to very sensitive information – but could handle it discreetly. Guys like that are very useful in our business and very hard to find. 'Course you have to watch them really fucking carefully, as one wrong move and they end up running the show.

That's how Frank Bennett started. He landed himself a job as a runner for the Nationalist Party back in the '50s

after the incumbent got his leg broken in a Gaelic match involving four of Bent's cousins. Then, slowly but surely, Frank set about acquiring the goods on every politician, fixer and bagman in North Derry (and large parts of Mid-Ulster to boot), and within three years, he'd been co-opted onto the council and was gunning for the MP's job. He'd have gone further than Westminster, too, if he hadn't been so greedy. Not that he was ever caught – no. He was far too cute for that. Rather, he worked out early that the higher up the tree you fly, the harder it is to feather your own nest. And if there was one thing that Frank Bent loved, it was a well-feathered nest.

OCTOBER

Dear Sue

Tuesday nights on my own at home are the worst – too early in the week to break our no-drinking pact, and all the weekend footie is over. Not that I'm happy at all with Sky losing half the matches to Setanta – that's another blasted £100 a year on the TV bill. Good job I'm a Catholic or I'd have to pay the licence as well.

As we expected, Frank Bent is going to let the bypass challenge proceed. He's got no option. But I just heard on the jungle drums he's already been back sniffing around your old pal Switchblade Vic, just in case the route gets shifted. Apparently, he's only asking Vic for an 8 per cent kickback from any of his land that is bought, instead of the 10 per cent he was screwing out of republican landowners for steering it their way. Very ecumenical indeed. But Brian McEldornie, a former IRA internee who coughed up close to £100,000 to oil Bent's wheels, has vowed to get his money back – to the penny. He will shake it out of him if needs be. And Bri is not a man I would like to have shaking me. Not as long as he's still holding on to two unlicensed shotguns . . .

Growing up in Derry, we learned to hate the faceless men – unionists all – who ran the town and sucked the people dry. Now, thanks to the Equality Agenda, we have our own Fenian variety, and I'm not sure I like them any better. I was about to say the only difference is that our lot don't wear poppies, but then I spotted a picture of Bent in this morning's *Derry Standard*. Fair play to young Devlin the photographer, he caught Bent just as he was trying to pull the overcoat across his poppy-laden lapel. That'll be worth a few ripe comments if he pops his head into the bash on Friday night.

Talking of which, my surprise party is no longer the complete surprise I had been anticipating. Brendy cracked and confessed all to me this morning when I asked him why my office was being billed for a six-piece showband. Apparently, Brendy lost his personal credit card during a bout of debauching at the weekend and had to stick me with the bill. (I think I just might know where to find it, though . . .)

Regardless, Brendy made me promise that I would act surprised when I walk into the darkened hall and you all leap out from behind the curtains. I told him I would do what I could – but if he really wanted to surprise me, why not have my girlfriend jump out of a cake. So, expect an interesting call over the next day or two. Oh, and all right – you can wear a garter.

I wouldn't worry too much about your mother, Sue. She's just protecting you. She knows the damage that consorting with the likes of me has done you already. Fair play to her, she's never made me feel anything but entirely welcome in her home – despite the fact that every time I visit Carsonville, you lose a hundred votes. If it has to be weekends away, it'll be weekends away. Sure the pair of us are on that new rural tourism committee and could probably wangle at least one free weekend a fortnight in exotic places like Stranocum and Spidéal. And as I've said many times before, girl, you look deadly in a tartan kilt.

Give me a bell when you get this and we'll discuss our escape strategy for Friday night.

Immense love
Shay

Carsonville
Greencastle

Dear Shay

Now, that's what I call a surprise party! You should have seen your face when you came into the hall, expecting to find all your nearest and dearest lining up to pay tribute to you, only for Brendy to tell you the night had been cancelled. Lack of interest . . . Only got four RSVPs . . . Really sorry, boss . . . Maybe in five years' time, when you're forty . . . They showed the whole thing on live video-link upstairs in the Castle Inn where the real party was waiting. We all thought you were going to cry. It was pitiful. I haven't laughed so hard since Paisley said he'd last a full term as First Minister.

Then, after you skulked across to the Castle Inn for a consolation drink, as we knew you would, Johnny the barman told you Father Giddens was out in the snug, hoping for a consult. So, sure as eggs, you legged it upstairs to hide – and crashed smack bang into the biggest surprise of your life. Four hundred people under a big 'Gotcha' banner. You were stitched up neater than a bishop's corpse.

Did I say biggest surprise of your life? That should of course read 'second biggest'. After you looked around the room, Brendy told you Danielle and I had gone to the Castle Inn in Dungiven by mistake and would be half an hour late. Five minutes later, I leapt out of the cake – and you nearly had to go home and change your trousers. God, you're easy meat, man. Talk about missing the obvious.

The party provided lots of evidence of our new political partnerships. Without giving too much away, let me just say that I will have plenty of company when I'm doing my penance in whatever ring of Protestant hell is reserved for those who fornicate with heathen Romanists. And the DUP hierarchy will be shocked to learn that not only is what Betty Biggard proposed to the new Sinn Féin chairman of Ballybockey a mortal sin, it is also illegal in all but one remote African village.

I loved your speech, by the way, even if you are a dreadful sentimentalist. My street cred as a hard-nosed Polly Prod took a terrible battering when you said all those wonderfully sweet things about me. Even Danielle had tears in her eyes – though, of course, she said it was out of mortification for you.

Anyway, Shay, for what it's worth, you are the first thing I think of in the morning, the last thing I think of at night – and most of what I think about in between. And no, I couldn't get through a day without you either. And yes, sometimes it's important to put these things on the record. So, you have me now, in black and white, for all time.

I love you forever and for always
Sue

Dear Assemblyman Gallagher

You mightn't remember me, but you taught me A-Level French at St Fiachra's College about seven years back, before you went into politics. Since then, I've got my degree and am now working as a computer engineer in Belfast.

The reason I'm contacting you is this: I've recently invented a piece of software that I think could be very useful to people like yourself in the political arena and wonder if you would be interested in helping me get it patented and marketed. I don't want to say too much about it in the letter, as it's cutting-edge stuff, but I can assure you it is the type of thing that could give you the edge in a tight contest.

I understand entirely if you're too busy to see me – a politician's schedule is hectic at the best of times, and I'd imagine yours is worse again with your wedding coming up. But I know you would be very interested in this idea, and it would be great to catch up on old times.

Yours
Patricia McAnarry

(You might remember me better as Porter-Eyes Patsy – you always said my eyes were as dark and soothing as the stout in Daddy's bar.)

Elmtree Apartments
Magee Road, Derry

Dear Shay

I saw the pictures from your party in this morning's paper and just wanted to write to wish you a very happy birthday.

You probably won't be able to place me, but you taught me French eight years ago; I was one of the top stream, Deirdre Docharty. (You used to think I was called Double D because of my initials, God bless your innocent heart.)

I always appreciated the way you took such an interest in our work and even organised out-of-hours grinds for my two pals and me coming up to the exams. It might sound silly, but I think the three of us really formed a strong personal bond with you.

I'm now a language teacher myself in Derry and am really enjoying passing on the benefits of your wisdom. (The other two top-streamers, by the way – Ciara O'Dowell and Frances McQuinn – are both in flying form: both lawyers and both married with a baby girl each.)

Anyway, the next time you're in Derry, the three of us would love to take you out to dinner as a thank you – and to wish you well on your chosen path. There's a lot of talk that you're going to run for Frank Bennett's seat when he steps down at the next general election. And we would all be willing to help out in whatever way we could. We're still your eager little beavers!

Yours truly
Double D
XOX

Parochial House
Chapel Road
Dunavady

Dear Shay

I had hoped to grab a word with you after Mass on Sunday, but you'd slipped out quicker than a four-letter word. Anyone would think you were trying to avoid me.

Regardless, this is important, as you'll already have gathered by the fact that I am writing this down and not risking either the phone or a visit to your office. (And just on that point, how is it that every time I have an appointment with you, Fianna Fáil headquarters ring with a pressing query, exactly seven minutes into our meeting?)

Anyway, you'll remember last year I warned you that the period leading up to his wedding is possibly the most dangerous and treacherous time of a man's entire life? Some women will do anything to derail a happy match – from baldly attempting to snatch the groom from under his new bride's nose to leading him astray just far enough so she can kiss and tell – and ruin the whole damn meeting.

You, my friend, I am astounded to admit, have played a blinder up until now. You have ably resisted the advances of five or six local Great White Hopes that I'm aware of, plus about a dozen more correspondents that young Brendan keeps tabs on for me.

Now, however, I have to alert you. You are in serious, serious danger. I have learned through a channel I cannot divulge (I need say no more) that a Southern newspaper is offering a five-figure sum for evidence of philandering – your philandering, that is.

It is no secret that you were a terrible gadabout before you settled with Sue (who we all agree is far too good for you). And for the past couple of weeks, a reporter from the *Dublin Daily* has been tracking down former St Fiachra's pupils, trying to get the goods on you.

As yet, he has been unable to pin down any proof of improper behaviour – largely because I kept such a tight bloody eye on you when you were in my employ, and also because Frances McQuinn was nineteen years old and an ex-student by all of six weeks when you 'legitimately' defiled her. If, however, there are any gaps in your résumé that you need to let us know about, now is the time to tell me.

In the meantime, be mindful that every woman who so much as nods her head or smiles in your direction is trying to set you up.

Yours sincerely
Monsignor N Giddens DD

PS You know, of course, to run this letter through the shredder immediately after reading it.

Dear Monsignor Giddens

Thank you most kindly for your letter. I have digested its contents most carefully and will act as you advise. As regards my résumé, there is virtually nothing of which I – or others – have not made you aware. MI5 wouldn't have a file on me the size of yours. Indeed, now I think of it, you might do well to get another bolt on your strong-room door.

In all sincerity, let me assure you that anything that rebounds on me at this juncture will be old news to yourself and will have absolutely no repercussions for the school. The McQuinn story, I should point out, is an urban myth – spread about by one of her 'friends', jealous because Frances got the highest mark in oral French. I may have been weak in my youth, Monsignor, but I wasn't an idiot. You would do well not to believe everything Sister Consumptive tells you as gospel.

You're right, of course, that I don't know how lucky I am and that Sue is far too good for me. But believe me, I would never do anything to damage what I have now.

Thank you again for your concern and your continued support. It is comforting for a man to know that he has friends who are watching out for him.

Yours respectfully
Shay

Memo: SG/BG

Brendy

Could you send Patricia McAnarry and Deirdre Docharty each a copy of the 'Fuck off, I'm not interested' letter? The softer version will be fine. Oh, and drop Father Giddens over a bottle of Black Bush to keep the old bastard civil. Put it on my account in the Castle offy – and don't try to stick me for a four-pack of Bacardi Breezers like you did the last day.

S

PS Father G has twigged to the Seven-Minute Maximum rule. Let's throw him out after three the next day so he'll appreciate us better down the line.

Constituency Office
Dunavady

Dear Sue

Just a brief note to warn you that the vultures are circling again. There's no new meat, though, I promise you. They're just hoping to pick over a few old corpses.

Old Giddens, the subtle bugger, is trying to blackmail me into supporting a new Over-21s Only rule for all Dunavady pubs by threatening to hand the McQuinn story over to some Dublin journalist. I actually agree with the ban; I've often said the teenagers here drink like children and the grown-ups drink like teenagers. But I could never support Father G's campaign publicly – not while I'm getting about 60 per cent of the under-25 vote in the town.

The McQuinn story, as you established yourself, was a heinous lie – and I'll close down any paper that tries to run it. But ever since Fianna Fáil announced they were organising up here, every Blue Shirt journalist in the Twenty-six Counties is busting his onions trying to get the dirt on me, the only legitimate FF'er north of the line. So, over the next few weeks, expect the usual quota of slappers lining up with their bare arses in the air to reveal how they once mounted my podium and rubbed my rosette.

I am terribly, terribly sorry about all this, and the embarrassment it causes you and Danielle – and even your mother. By way of excuse, all I can say is that up until Uncle Shay died six years ago, I never imagined that I'd spend my life as anything but a private citizen. And I behaved as such.

If it all becomes too much, remember I gave you your 'get-out' card a long time ago, Sue, and will understand entirely any time you want to play it – even if I do die of a broken heart. I don't deserve you, Sue. But the thing is, neither does anybody else. So, if you can bear with me, I'll be eternally grateful. (Which, let's be honest, I am anyway.)

If it's of any solace, the tawdry stuff should slow up when we get married. Newspaper reporters tend to leave us (former) players alone once we're safely strung up on a butcher's hook like the rest of them.

I'll talk to you when you get this – and maybe meet up for a chat tomorrow night.

Love you always
Shay

Members' Offices
Stormont

Dear Shay, you asshole

As I told you last night, I knew what I was getting when I took that diamond ring. That's why the vows won't read 'for richer or for better'.

I'll not pretend I'm not annoyed – but only because I know you're not that guy any more. Though be mindful, I remember that guy and will cut off his man-bits if he ever resurfaces in any guise. I didn't like him, Shay – I certainly didn't love him – and I don't like being reminded of his existence. For the minute, however, I can square it all off in my head by contenting myself that he's a whole different person from the one I am in love with now.

I still don't know why the papers feel obliged to drag me into this and trot out every stereotype about red hair known to man. I swear to God, if one more reporter ever refers to me as your 'hot-tempered' or 'feisty' fiancée, I will personally batter him to a mushy pulp. And not in a playful way either.

On the plus side, Danielle reckons the redtops are doing you a big favour, particularly with female voters. As long as they think your zipper's still shaky, your vote's going to shoot through the roof.

As we were discussing, you could make life a lot easier for yourself by throwing in your lot with one of the bigger parties. There's always that greater degree of protection when you've got a team minding your back. The Stoops would seem to be your natural home; and given their deathless foreplay with FF, you could be a de facto member before too long anyway. Only two problems with that: first you'll have to get another wife to take to party conferences, as there's no way I'm sitting through Mark Durkan's speeches; and second, as soon as Gerry Diver gets off the SDLP subs' bench, you'll no longer be the prettiest boy in the room.

If you were studying the formbook, however, Sinn Féin might be a better bet for you. They would guarantee you a free shot at Bent's seat next time out, and the Shinners still retain enough scary-bastard mystique to intimidate editors into not publishing scandal about their members. The difficulty here is that Fianna Fáil will disown you – and you'll betray your proud family heritage. Oh, and everyone south of the border will be convinced you are a fuck-witted commie. (Talking of which, who in-under Jesus thought it would be a good idea to put Gerry A in a head-to-head debate with McDowell? They'd have done him less harm if they'd stuck him in a snuff film with a cross on his back.)

Your third option is for Fianna Fáil to start up independently in the North with you as their poster boy. That way, you could salvage your last remaining shards of political integrity, strong-arm a few quid seed money from De Party, and have protection aplenty, at least in the Free State. Your main dilemma here is that you might have to learn to be a true leader of men instead of shooting from the sidelines. And we both know that day is a little bit away just yet.

Anyway, there's lots to think about there but, sure, there's lots of time.

I'll close now, having forgiven you utterly. Though can I just point out, as a purely selfless gesture, that there is a beautifully slender pearl choker in Faller's window display in Derry, at a ridiculously low price. And while I would never presume to play upon your (richly deserved) guilt, it might make you feel more secure in your own mind if I were to accept – nay, graciously accept– such a surprise from your hand.

I love you, you bloody idiot
Sue

PS I'm sure I needn't remind you that an £800 chain is very light in terms of conscience money. My mother took a Jag from my father for his last affair. (I, as we have already established, would take the same Jag and drive it over your torn-off testicles . . . XOX)

To: The Eyrie
Dunavady

Dear Mr Gallagher

I think we have our little pervert bang to rights. On Saturday night, your associate Brendan was caught by our unit, committing lewd and unbecoming conduct in a public place. After tracking him for four hours, I collared him and a fellow violator in a remote section of an underground car park, clearly contravening public decency. But my sergeant – a godless Englishman – decided not to prosecute and let them away without even a caution. He was clearly wrong, however, as you will see from the three photographs enclosed in which the pair can clearly be seen holding hands, kissing and, well, canoodling.

I trust you will act immediately on this cast-iron evidence before your PA gets a chance to commit any other embarrassments in your name.

Your friend and guardian
Serpico

PERSONAL
To: Chief Superintendent Edward O'Conway
Commander
Strand Road PSNI, Derry
(CC Brendan Gallagher)

Ed, a chara

I attach a copy of my morning mail. Please locate this headcase and batter the tar out of him. There's at least one novel approach with a truncheon I can recommend.

See you at the match on Sunday.

Slán go fóill
Shay

Memo: BG/SG

Shay

Re: our conversation a couple of weeks back.

This neck of the woods is becoming a bit stifling for a spirited young man like myself. And while I really appreciate your assurances that there'll be no more harassment, I think it's time I spread my wings a little. I also know that I am in danger of becoming an embarrassment to my parents and yourself.

Marty Doolin, a cousin of my partner's, has just opened a new dance club in Dublin and is looking for a couple of duty managers. And we both think it's time. So, I'm going to hit the road just as soon as you can get a new man/woman/pillow-biter installed here. I've loved every minute of working with you, Shay, but the problem with small towns is that no matter how much you dress them up, they'll always be small towns.

Brendan

Memo: SG/BG

Brendan

I do hope you know you're breaking my heart, and not in any pansy way. You'll be a terrible loss to me personally and professionally. And seriously, man, an embarrassment? To me?? Did you READ the weekend papers? The very worst you'd do is take some heat off me.

In all sincerity, though, you're dead right to try something new. You're far too smart to grow old answering my phones. In saying that, anytime you want to come back – anytime – just call me.

Shay

PRIVATE AND CONFIDENTIAL
Chief Superintendent's Office
Strand Road PSNI, Derry

Shay, a chara

Didn't take us long to find him – the only cop in the building who insists on wearing a little Jesus Is In Me badge on his cap.

With your permission, we'd like to try and re-educate him rather than sack him outright. The latter would be very messy. And we'd only end up handing him a big bundle of money he doesn't deserve just so he'll fuck off quietly.

As and from tomorrow, Serpico will become deputy liaison officer with the travelling community for the entire county. And we've made it clear to him that he'll be run out the door if we get one single, solitary allegation of discrimination. And to keep him honest, we've let the boyos in on the secret – and given them his home and mobile phone numbers.

Any further torture you can think of would be most welcome.

Beidh ár lá linn
Ed

We had to send Serp a message, if only for Brendy's sake, but my respect for him was growing rapidly. I could sense his tremendous determination to succeed at all costs, and he desperately wanted to feature on our radar. Most of all, I was more and more convinced that he could be useful to us. Very useful.

People who keep animals as pets miss the whole point. A tame poodle, while pretty to look at, serves no purpose. Much better by far a beast who can earn his keep. A properly trained dog can save your life with a timely warning; he can terrify your enemies with one snarl – or he can rip their cheeks off with a judicious bite. And I knew from day one that Serpico could be such an animal.

Shay's female difficulties were a lot more worrying to me. He had spent the previous five years fending off round after round of cute little long-legged vultures – but now the attacks seemed to be more concerted. His loyalty to Sue was beyond question, but none of us is immune. Any man can let his guard down after a couple of drinks. And the whole situation was compounded by the fact that he and Sue were apart for four nights a week.

In normal circumstances, you'd just keep a tight eye on things and hope for the best. But he was just so damn attractive – so young, so rich, so powerful and very, very charming. And unfortunately, he also had the libido of a seventeen-year-old man-child who'd just discovered Viagra . . .

NOVEMBER

Dear Sue

Not quite as bad as I feared – the tabloids, I mean, not you. But I've a feeling that story about how I time my three-minute egg is going to hound me forever. And no, it wasn't a bit fair of them to dress you up with a stopwatch and a chef's hat. Anyway, thanks for punishing me precisely the appropriate amount and not a bit more. (You're not anywhere near as hardboiled as they make you out . . . Just my little yolk there . . . I'll stop now.)

The press, as we're all learning, have too little to do now the war's over. Time was, they could just follow the loud bangs. Now they have to justify their existence, and scandal is the big seller. It's not necessarily the media's fault either. The *Derry Standard* editor, Stan Stevenson, told me he's guaranteed a circulation drop of 500 copies if he headlines the front page with a political story or anything else remotely worthy. The public prefer gossip and innuendo over substance, so the Fourth Estate feel obliged to pander. Worst of all is the recent influx of 'Party' pages – acre upon acre of shaven-headed, nipple-pierced oiks, leglessly celebrating one of their number's coming-of-age or impending nuptials. And the fellas' bashes are even worse.

Coverage of our Stormont work is really limited – unless, of course, you put your foot in something. The *Standard*, fair play to them, did, however, carry an extended report questioning Frank Bent's wearing of the poppy, on the grounds that while nationalists might have forgiven the British army for what they did here, they certainly don't forget it.

We all know that Frank is only prostituting himself to keep in with the real powers that be. His argument is that if it helps him network better with British money, and bring British money to our borough, then what the hell. But he'd do well to heed the words of our most eloquent dissident leader, Malky McTobeen, as quoted in the piece. He opined: 'Somebody should plug the c*** then bury him under a field of f***ing poppies – see how he likes that.' Never mince your words, Malky. Tell us what you really think.

I actually got it in the ear from both a Shinner and a Stoop for declining an invitation to the commemorations at the War Memorial. There's a growing perception that this is now a cross-community love-in and only bigots won't attend. Except, of course, that is complete bollocks. My army and my country did not fight in the two world wars. And I have no affiliation to those who did.

Moreover, while I cherish your lot just as much as the next guy (and indeed, sometimes a good deal more passionately), I would never expect you to wear the Easter lily – or fire the starting gun at the anti-internment commemorations. Respecting diversity means just that – it doesn't mean living in the other guy's skin.

For all that, I love the fresh poppies you and Danielle have been wearing this year. As a symbol of remembrance, a real live flower is so much more powerful. And I honestly think it's a pity that you lost a couple of great-uncles in World War One. The world, and particularly this backward little corner of it, could do with a lot more of your kind.

I'll go now, content that I've done enough to provoke a letter back – or at the very least a long stream of telephonic invective.

Love always
Shay

PS The pearl choker looked perfect. I felt like Dracula – I couldn't keep my eyes off that lovely white neck of yours all night.

Carsonville
Greencastle

Dear Shay

At least you're right about the choker – it does make my neck look damn fine. And while I agree it's outrageous you're still getting punished for your ancient history, can I forewarn you now that Faller's have a matching pair of earrings for the next time your youthful sins return to bite you on the ass.

Needless to say, you're way off the mark on the poppy issue.

46

Yes, we all know that Frank Bent is a panderer, and we all know what he's at by wearing his little buttonhole – and not one of us is fooled. We hate him every bit as much as you did those trendy English republicans who used to appear on the platform in your civil rights campaigns. You lauded them publicly as liberal British heroes. Then the minute their backs were turned, you damned them privately as MI5 and MI6 spies. It's one of the great commonalities of our two communities – our ability to weed out and put to death anyone who smells like a wrong egg.

Where your thinking falls down is on why I, or my family, wear poppies. It's nothing to do with two fallen relics whom none of us ever met, or the commemoration of a war that quite frankly you couldn't get five people to support if you mooted it in parliament today. It's not about triumphalism or celebrating our army's all-too-rare successes over your terrorist friends during the past thirty years. I wear the flower because I recognise it for what it is – the last tangible symbol of our link to Britain. Our soldiers are gone, our flags have been taken down, our loyalty oaths have been struck out, and the odds are if you throw a stone at a police patrol these days, you're going to hit a Papist (even if he is Polish).

The poppy is all we have left. Our sense of Britishness has been replaced with a new anodyne Northern Irishness, which amounts to not mentioning the war and trying not to gauge how close our neighbour's eyes are to each other. For culture, instead of looking to the empire which established us as its colony, we're being told to embrace Ulster-Scots – a hideous, mocking joke invented by cynics to satisfy the checks and balances of a few Irish-hating bigots.

The poppy allows us to share in something we used to feel a valued part of; it allows us to pretend, for a short time, that we have a home. And if a Stoop or Shinner feels enough genuine empathy to wear one and to say to us, sincerely and without hypocrisy, 'we respect your heritage', then let them wear it in peace, free from your snippy gibes.

The problem with symbols, as I've said to you many times before, is that they never mean the same thing to two different people. My purple flower is a dissident's purple target. You, of course, Shay, never wear symbols at all – neither the lily nor the shamrock nor the poppy. And you spin it wonderfully as a virtue. Only problem with that is you can't always run away from what you believe in.

Lecture over. And don't fret, you're not in any more trouble. I love the fact that we can be honest enough to talk about these things – and that you never get offended when I point out how stupid, ill-informed and pig-ignorant you're being.

I'm very sorry to hear you'll be losing Brendy, by the way. I'll have to find another way of keeping tabs on you. Seriously, though, if I were in your shoes I'd be throwing bagfuls of money at him to make him stay. Not that it'll work, though – he's right about small towns and small minds. If you like, I'll give you a hand picking a new assistant – Tommy Bowtie has me well apprised of the criteria you normally use. (Is it true you only gave Brendy the job because Miss Drumcastle with the forty-inch legs turned out to be three months pregnant?)

I love you always
Sue

To: The Eyrie
Dunavady

Dear Mr Gallagher

I wish to apologise profusely for my earlier letters to you, which may have wrongly implied that I was pursuing a discriminatory agenda against your assistant. Brendan is a fine, upstanding pillar of society, but because of his particular predilections, I can understand entirely how he might have felt I was exceeding the legitimate pursuit of my duties.

My writing to you about the matter was merely intended as a warning – and not as a threat. Just as I wish to alert you now that you, yourself, are in serious danger of reaping the dividends of what could be wrongly perceived as indiscretions.

It has come to my attention that twice this week, and once last, you were sighted leaving a very comely young woman's home at a very late hour. Furthermore, the woman is a married Sinn Féin politician, whose husband spends a lot of time away on business.

Now, while I am absolutely certain that no impropriety took place – not given your very public devotion to your fiancée, Miss Susan McEwan – can I please advise you, as an ally, to be more discreet in your movements.

Your friend
Serpico

Confidential Memo: SG/Tommy Bowtie

Tommy

As attached. Looks like the start of a shakedown. Doesn't mention photos – but you can be sure the fucker has them. Shit. I'm sorry. Really, really sorry.

Please reply soonest. (Could you clear the decks for tonight?)

Shay

Constituency Office
Dunavady

Dear Sue

I'm just off the phone to you and want to thank you again for being so understanding about me breaking our date tonight – I love you more than ever. I know you were looking forward to seeing Bruce Willis this evening, but I promise you that this weekend you'll see more action than *Die Hard One* through *Four* – the uncut versions. I realise our Wednesdays should be sacrosanct – but Tommy Bowtie really has a bee in his bonnet about this bypass issue, so I'd better humour him.

I was thinking about your offer to help me get a new PA – and it could actually be a good idea. But I'll have you know that all those stories about my casting couch are completely untrue.

Brendy got his position by merit alone. And that *Sunday News* article about me and my first secretary was very much exaggerated. I never so much as stood on top of that filing cabinet to change a light bulb – let alone attempted what they were suggesting.

Brendy himself might sit in on the interviews as well. He's spent the past two years watching my back and has become very good at sniffing out troublemakers. He'll also be training up whoever gets the job, explaining what calls I will and will not take, and the importance of updating the Lunatics' List on a daily basis.

Frank Bent's just off Radio Foyle, where he's been ripping the back off me for helping stall the bypass. The interviewer, fair play to her, kept irking him about how I was his possible successor and that it would be left to me to clean up any mess he left. Eventually, his mask slipped big style and he called me an 'enemy of the borough', which should be worth a thousand votes on polling day. I'd only go forward if I got a clear run (from our lot) and, as you know, that's looking less likely by the hour. I would never run to get beat.

I love you more with each passing day
Shay

Confidential Memo: Tommy/SG

Shay

A hundred times out of a hundred I'd advise you to confess all and turn this guy in to his bosses. But this time, I'm not so sure. You might have to meet him halfway. Call into the office after tea and we'll go into the closed room for a confab. Can I also advise you, as your lawyer, that you're a complete fucking dimwit.

TB

Oh, and break off all contact with AK forever. Did you hear me? FOREVER.

Confidential Memo: Ned Broy/Ailis Kernanny

Ailis

Your place is being watched. We're going to have to find another way of doing this. Suggest calling everything off for a couple of weeks at least. Many apologies.

S

Parochial House
Dunavady

Dear Shay

I'm corresponding to your home address, as I have growing doubts about the wisdom of sending mail to your office. That secretary of yours has such a busy little tongue on him. It's about time he stopped running to clubs in Derry and settled down with a good woman.

Anyhow, to the reason I'm writing. There's a policeman who was round to see me this morning, asking questions about yourself and Ailis Kernanny – and wondering if there's any history between you. I told him nothing, Shay. But there aren't five people in the borough who don't know the truth – and there aren't five in the county who can keep their mouth shut.

You're playing with fire here, man. You are going to get burnt. Stop now, in the name of God, before you get out of your depth entirely.

Yours
Monsignor N Giddens DD

Hi Shay

The cops are telling everyone you're back in play – and have been spotted buzzing around the porch of a certain lonely lady. I thought you swore that if you ever went off the rails again, you'd be sure to come crashing into me?

I realise you need to be discreet – now you're such a major public figure and all – but as I said before, my back door is always open (to you at least).

Pity things didn't work out with Sue. She was lovely – but a little bit too much Red Riding Hood for a wolf like you. Talking of which, any time you fancy a howl, just scratch on my gate.

Love always
Jacqui XOX

PS Sorry about that egg-timer story, by the way. I told them four times it was a twenty-minute pizza. But you know reporters!

Memo: SG/Tommy Bowtie

Tommy

I think your first instinct was right and I should come clean. I know we agreed last night we'd wait and see what Serpico produced, but the innuendo is already doing me serious damage. Let me know what you think. Soonest.

S

Darling Shay

You really are the most marvellous man in the world. Thank you so much for the earrings. I feel like a Greek goddess. I can't wait to see you tomorrow night to model them for you personally.

You make me so happy, Shay.

Sue
XXXXXXX

The Eyrie
Dunavady

Dear Monsignor Giddens

Take a breath and think about this. You are a smart, reasonable man – and always afforded me the benefit of the doubt, even when I didn't deserve it, as I do now.

Do you seriously think I would risk my personal happiness and professional career to fool around with a married woman? A married woman who, I might add, saw right through me fifteen years ago when I failed miserably in my attempts to wrest her from the clutches of big Kernanny. She adores her husband. I adore Sue.

This policeman who visited you has an agenda to get me. Pure and simple. I am a politician and my opponents will use what they can to undermine me – sometimes even lies.

I am not the guy I was five years ago, Father. I am not the guy your niece hated so much that she bought a box of Labrador pups, named them all Shay, then systematically neutered each and every one. That guy is a dead Shay. He no longer breathes. He has ceased to be.

I worked out a long time ago that Sue is every woman I ever wanted to be with – my Lauren Bacall, Marilyn Monroe and Sandra Bullock all rolled into one. And there is no more likelihood of me blowing that than there is of Brendy settling down with a good woman, Father – so get over it.

Do me a favour. Trust me on this. Don't feed into this copper's dirty little blackmail game. Accept the fact I'm being honest, tell the doubters you believe in me, and I'll not let you down.

Yours respectfully
Shay

Memo: Tommy/SG

Shay

I hope you've managed to square off Father Giddens by now. He's got a mouth on him the size of Banagher Dam. And just as leaky, too. I still think we should brazen this out. They've got nothing.

TB

Constituency Office
Dunavady

Dear Sue

Best weekend ever. Thank you for thanking me for thanking you. Honest to God, if you'd thanked me any more I'd have needed a saline drip. (Though if you ever fancy a little pearl belly-button ring to complete the set, just let me know . . .)

Glad I got my head cleared, as this morning it was straight back into the murky morass that is politics North Derry style. Ed O'Conway phoned me at 9.30 am and told me to expect a visitor from the 'security services', and, sure enough, half an hour later, a guy arrived and told Brendy he'd been given a 'priority' appointment.

I have to say, their spooks are so much better, i.e. less obvious, than the old school. This guy, who called himself Jack White, looked like a forty-year-old plumber, right down to the porn-star moustache and saggy jeans with a fetching view of his ample arse. Put him in any social club in the Falls or Sandy Row and you'd lose him in the wallpaper straight away.

Mind like a trap, though, and the vocabulary of a Trinity scholar. He knew all about my previous difficulties (and yours), not that his visit had anything to do with them. He's worried about dissident republicans in the borough – reckons they're about to make some bold, i.e. murderous, statement about the PSNI.

I don't sit on any of the policing partnerships or liaison groups, so Jack's not too concerned about me – this time. But his information is that the local 'Coca Colas', as he called them (The Real Thing . . .) are intent on sending a serious message to all us Fenian lackeys who support the new policing arrangements. And given that the spooks are running one in every two dissidents on the island, you've got to imagine our man knows what he's talking about.

The main target would seem to be Bent; the dissidents always hated his toadying. Though it's also just possible they'd try their luck with one of the senior SDLP officers. They don't have the Niagaras to take on a real live Shinner. I just hope Mr White can make a timely intervention before they do any harm (unless, of course, it is Bent – in which case I hope they snare the bad guys on their way back home).

Bent, by the by, is having another rattle at me in today's *Derry Standard*. He's saying I have cost the borough 300 jobs by delaying the bypass – and that the reason they (he) didn't consider any other route is that it wasn't 'topographically' possible. This from a man who would drive a road through the fires of hell if he thought Beelzebub would give him his 10 per cent kickback. I'm going to have to take a slap back at him, if only for form's sake – though I hate giving the bloody crook the publicity.

The ad for my new Brendy went in the paper this morning as well. I didn't specify who it was for – just left a box number. Much safer. This time, I'll be spared a mountain of middle-aged women's underclothing and some equally graphic photos (not all of which, I later learned, were Photoshopped). Ah, the perils of a young Gladstone.

It'd be great this time to get someone who can spell – and maybe do a bit of PR work. Brendy is the best eyes, ears and young defender a man could ever have, but he's got all the syntax of a pre-1994 DUP councillor – or indeed SF councillor. I'm not prejudiced, just grammatically intolerant. I'd poach your Lindsay in a heartbeat, except, of course, that would conflict with your 'no smoking-hot babes who fancy the boss' rule.

I'm sorry I'm so giddy today. I'm just about to meet with a guy who wants to blackmail me – and I'm thinking how best to end his life. More of which anon.

I love you to the moon and back
Shay

To: Stan Stevenson
Editor, Derry Standard
Barkley Industrial Park
Dunavady

Dear Stan

Enclosed find my reply to The Right Honourable Francis Bennett. I've taken your advice and not included claims about his highly inappropriate love of sheep. You're right – it might reflect badly on the borough as a whole. (Especially after those photos of Councillor Colloway.)

Seriously, though, I kept it legally very tight – didn't state anything I couldn't substantiate. The last thing you want to do is make a mistake and give the fucker either a right to reply or, worse again, the chance to sue you. Tommy Bowtie reckons the letter's airtight, but you might want to run it past your legal people, too, just in case.

Thanks for the tip-off about a 'cash trail', by the way. It'll put Bennett out of the picture a whole lot quicker than the consultation would have – and also let us have a real discussion about the bypass.

See you in the Castle Inn for a late one on Thursday night – I'm buying.

Shay

FOR IMMEDIATE PUBLICATION

Constituency Office of Shay Gallagher MLA
Main Street, Dunavady

Dear Editor

I note from recent editions of your periodical that Frank Bennett MP seems to believe that I personally – and not the Department of Environment – am responsible for his current woes.

Mr Bennett has now accused me twice of pursuing an agenda to 'derail' the road he so carefully planned out on the back of his Cornflakes packet with his granddaughter's crayon set. He further suggests that any route other than the one he drew up would be impossible to construct.

With all due respect, Mr Bennett, it's a mountain we're going over – not a volcano. I think what you meant to say is that it would be impossible to construct a route that would prove more profitable for Vady Construction – the only contractors allowed to tender for the project – of which, incidentally, you, Mr Bennett, are a registered shareholder.

You should be careful, Mr Bennett, not to interfere with the new and impartial consultation process, which was agreed following the recent High Court challenge to your route. You have already prejudiced one process by not allowing any consultation at all to take place – you cannot be allowed to subvert another.

The reason for your panic at this time, however, is that vesting orders which were to be made, purchasing the land of more than a score of your constituents, will not now be honoured.

And while this is a matter for the Department of Environment, several of your constituents (I am reliably informed) have launched a class action against Vady Construction for failure to deliver on a contract. Specifically, these farmers are asserting that they were given cast-iron guarantees their land would be purchased for the road – guarantees over and above those given by the Department.

Now, far be it from me to suggest that you, Mr Bennett, or your agents, were responsible for issuing these cast-iron guarantees on behalf of Vady Construction. You should, however, be aware that I have received evidence from one of my constituents, regarding the recent vesting of his land, which I intend to lodge with the hearings when they resume next Monday. This evidence, I believe, will help the panel decide conclusively on whether the bypass route could ever proceed as originally (mis-) planned.

I look forward to seeing you at the Town Hall on Monday to view the evidence for yourself, Mr Bennett – that is, if you can take the time out from your gentlemen's clubs in London to deal with the most urgent matter to affect our borough in fifty years.

Yours sincerely
Shay Gallagher,
Member of the Legislative Assembly for North Derry

PRIVATE AND CONFIDENTIAL
From the Office of the Right Honourable Francis Bennett MP
House of Commons
Westminster

Dear Mr Gallagher

Further to our weekend discussion, I have instructed my counsel to support your proposal to disqualify the formerly preferred Dunavady bypass route from inclusion in any further consultation process. I accept unreservedly that the route is no longer viable.

The hearings will now be postponed until after Christmas, when, I am given to understand, they will be wound up. At that stage, I will, of course, also be most happy to second your Assembly motion to shelve all plans for a bypass for five years.

I would further like to thank you for bringing those matters to which you alluded in the press to my private attention, discreetly. I only regret that I was not made aware of this evidence sooner. As you say, we may all have been too hasty in our need to keep up with the bigger players.

Yours sincerely
Frank Bennett

Carsonville
Greencastle

My darling clever boy

Remind me never to fall out with you. I just wish I'd been there to see Bent's face when you presented him with Donal McFulton's box file. Who would have believed Donal would have been so devious as to photocopy fifteen hundred £10 notes before handing them over as a bribe? And who'd have thunk Bent would be so dim as to lodge the self-same notes with Dunavady Credit Union – particularly when Tommy Bowtie is the honorary treasurer?

I think you were right, though, to give Bennett a graceful retreat. You own him, now and forever. And by not bringing it into the public domain or the courts, it means the idiot farmers will get their money returned immediately – plus another 10 per cent for goodwill on top. They'll still lose out on the land sales, though, and I'd imagine you are going to catch some of the blame for that – but you're talking twenty or thirty votes there, as opposed to the thousand extra you're going to get from all those excitable young cuddies back in the town who think you're Wyatt Earp.

I wouldn't be too concerned over Bent's threats to you either, Shay. It was just his temper talking after you sliced him open. And yes, I know this cop is worrying you, trying to dredge up your past. But since you've been with me, you've kept your undercarriage very clean (for a low-down, dirty dog).

Your mistake with Serpico has been keeping him outside the tent. Much better to have a guy like that working for you than urinating all over the sleeping bags. Why not ask him to do you a private favour – get the goods on Bent, that sort of thing? Make him feel useful – valued, even. All at one level of deniability, though, as I'd imagine our man will eventually implode, taking his nearest and dearest – and all those who couldn't run away quick enough – along with him. But there's no point in stressing out over him. In all the time I've known you, this is the first time you've not been able to sleep over worrying about something. Normally at night you just say some wonderful things to me, whisper a silent prayer and roll over – and that's it for eight hours until you look round again with an expectant smile on your face . . .

I talked to the builders this morning, and the house will be finished on 1 February. So you'll have exactly six months to get it perfect for me. (We return from our honeymoon – and officially move in together – on 1 August.) Sorry you're not hanging on to The Eyrie; it's one fine bachelor pad, but we're in enough debt without retaining that mortgage. My mother, bless her, still can't understand why I'm forsaking her unheated, five-bedroom, one-bathroom, nineteenth-century wind tunnel for a mere Jacuzzi, mini-cinema and basement bar. Though, interestingly, she's already dropped hints about coming up to the new place for a visit. You are a living saint for adding on the granny flat and calling it a visitors' apartment. Really. Sometimes, I honestly think you might just be good enough for me.

I don't mind at all moving into North Derry either, not so long as I can keep my office at Mum's. Fair enough, the cattle up your parts might look a little more Fenian than I'm used to, but the security threat is all but gone. Danielle is also not protesting anywhere near as much as you'd expect from a teenage grunge queen. Again, what a masterstroke – a media room with her own private entrance. I take my hat off to you (and indeed, many other things).

I love you dearly, Shay
Sue

PS Sorry I can't make Tuesday night but I've been invited to the DUP dinner-dance and protocol demands I'd better show my face. Hate the things with a passion at the best of times, but this one will be even worse as we'll be forced to eat the steak dinner with forks only. (Apparently all the knives have been lodged in the Paisleys' backs.)

The Eyrie
Dunavady

Dear Sue

Bent will have his revenge. The bastard is spreading lies about me via our pal Serpico, who, as I guessed, is in his pay. But our darling parliamentary representative is not only hoping to discredit me, he's also looking to have me whacked – he's putting it about that I'm having an affair with Ailis Kernanny, the Shinner councillor! Ailis, you'll recall, is married to Daithi Kernanny, the retired Ballysaggart Sniper, who could still blow the arse wings off a horsefly from two hundred paces.

I've spoken to Bent this morning and warned him if I find he'd anything to do with these rumours, I'd personally give a few un-retired paramilitaries the floor maps to his home and the plans to his garden. He pleaded innocence, of course. Injured innocence, even. But I know the nature of the beast. He's so twisted that even when he's caught bang to rights he can't stop himself from lying.

Ultimately, though, why I am writing is to tell you this: things might be about to get sordid again. I have thrown out one Hail Mary, which may buy me a bit of grace. (Full story another time.) But I want you to know, one last time, that I am giving you full licence to walk away now. No strings.

Let me stress, this is not about me being heroic. It's rather about me not wanting to damage two careers. Mine could be about to take a hit – a serious hit. I've spent five years living down my playboy youth and could wind up looking like a middle-aged fool who couldn't outgrow his inner teen-pervert.

The only thing I can assure you is this, Sue. You have my word – as the man who loves you more than anything in this world, who would die happy if only I could make you happy – I didn't touch Ailis. No matter what appears in any paper, please believe this – even if you finally realise you're better rid of me.

I love you with every fibre of my being
Shay

To: The Eyrie
Dunavady

Dear Mr Gallagher

Can I just say I am thrilled at the offer to become your personal assistant at Stormont. As I said to your agent, Mr McGinlay, I have training in media and am also exceptionally well connected across all branches of the security forces. I would expect that my salary would reflect the fact that I have an honours degree and also carry a licensed firearm. You're getting two for one, Mr Gallagher – a PA and a bodyguard.

Yours
Grayson McKeepney BA (Hons)

PS You can still call me Serpico – it'll be our in-joke.

Memo: SG/Tommy Bowtie

Tommy

I can hardly believe it! You're a fucking angel. He's climbed on board. And he's literate. I'll be the envy of Stormont. Talk about win-win. Tell him he can start in the New Year.

Shay

It was a risk, of course, a terrible risk as it turned out. But Sue had hit the nail right on the head – as long as Serpico was inside the tent, Shay would stay dry. We checked him out first, naturally, and knew well that he would be coming with his own agenda. But we also were aware that like any highly trained animal, he would be totally loyal to us, as long as we were of use to him.

The Kernanny connection, however, was an enormously dangerous one, given Ailis's history with Shay and her notoriously jealous husband. Truth be told, she would never have figured on my own Christmas wish-list, but she had that peculiarly vibrant shade of red hair that always put a shake in Shay's hand and a stammer in his mouth.

I warned him and warned him and warned him till my throat was sore. Daithi Kernanny was a guy who, quite literally, had spent his life shooting first and asking questions later. But Shay wasn't going to let some frustrated middle-aged lawyer like me knock him off his game. He had his plan and by God, he was going to stick with it.

DECEMBER

Memo: SG/BG

Brendy

Just to confirm that I would like the office to be closed all day tomorrow, 5 December, for Frank Bennett's funeral. Could you stick a sign to that effect in the front window? Make it sound regretful – but not too sad.

Thanks
Shay

Memo: SG/Tommy Bowtie

Tommy

I need to pick that fine brain of yours. Fr Giddens is insisting on me doing the eulogy. He feels I'm his only chance of not hearing the words 'fucker', 'going', 'straight', 'to' and 'hell', at the graveside. The Shinners laughed out loud when he suggested one of them; they told him they're only sorry there's a ceasefire in place so the dissidents were able to beat them to the kill. The Stoops said they would do the speech, but on condition they got 10 per cent of the collection plate. And even Giddens recognised that as sarcasm. So, it's down to yours truly.

Is there any way it's possible to turn this into an opportunity – without saying something that's going to get me planted in the hole next door to Frank?

Shay

Memo: Tommy/SG

Shay

Call round after five and we'll kick a few ideas around.

Just off the phone to Ed O'Conway. They're fairly definite maverick republicans were behind the hit, though which ilk, they're not sure. They've had three different claims. The shotgun, apparently, had never been used before – at least not on humans. The cops are curious as to how the shooter knew Bent would be in his back garden. But as I told Ed, everyone in the borough knows that Bent spent his Saturdays working with his roses.

By the way, I'd a great time in Dublin at the weekend. Thanks for arranging those tickets for us all to the game on Saturday – I never knew you and Sue were such rugby fans.

See you this evening.
Tommy

To: The Eyrie
Dunavady

Dear Assemblyman Gallagher

Just a quick note to sympathise with you on the loss of your dear colleague Francis. Despite your political differences, I know from our private conversation the high esteem in which you held him.

I was very distressed to learn, however, that some of your opponents have already started a whispering campaign against you, suggesting that you were in some way in cahoots with Mr Bennett's cold-blooded killers. Their jealousy, however, will rebound on them, I assure you. While I realise I won't be in situ until January, I am already making very discreet inquiries (in the throes of my current day job) on your behalf. And I can tell you that Chris Caddle of Sinn Féin and the SDLP's Barney Deverry have both been recorded making gloating and triumphalist comments about your poor colleague's brutal murder. Tape-recorded, that is.

Public houses are a copper's godsend, Mr Gallagher. And publicans are always anxious to keep in with the local constabulary. They need us to keep their licences – and to keep order. Always remember that. You can never be too careful. Your enemies have eyes and ears everywhere.

Finally, while I would never wish to exceed my brief, can I also inform you, most confidentially, that my former unit is investigating the possibility that two local farmers who had financial dealings with Mr Bennett over the bypass development may not have been where they said they were on Saturday afternoon past.

Yours respectfully
Serpico

Memo: Ned Broy/Ailis

Ailis

Looks like our little trouble has fizzled out. We'll give it another week or so, then hook up again. Try not to shake my hand at the funeral tomorrow. That's one picture we don't want appearing in the press anytime soon.

S

The Eyrie
Dunavady

Dear Sue

Thanks for coming today – it was so comforting to see one person in the cortège who wasn't there to get their face on TV.

Even if you were the most stylish mourner by a mile. A black French beret on copper-red hair. Wee Brendy said he'd almost hop back over the fence for you. (Be sure and bring it with you on Friday night.)

Tommy Bowtie helped me with the oration, by the way. And thank God for him, too – he could make Britney Spears look like the Virgin Mary.

It would have been tempting to take the easy option and launch into a panegyric on Bennett's virtues. He did all the right things for the optics: he sat in the front row at Mass; never cheated on that grasping harpy of a wife (or at least not after that beating she gave him the first time); and he always espoused the non-violent path to political progress (never once going beyond blackmail, threats or psychological intimidation).

But ultimately, a love-in would have been pointless – and not a sinner or Shinner there would have bought it. Not even his family. It was much better to acknowledge his flaws first day. Bent was a cynical operator who, like many politicians, had gone into the business to make himself rich. The plus side of this was that he didn't keep it all for himself and made quite a few people around him rich as well. Which is why he was elected three times to represent us in the House of Commons.

Under his reign, we built an industrial park, three other major factories, two bridges and a dozen assorted hotels. He was damn good for tourism – and never missed a chance to tell prospective visitors or investors how incredibly scenic the borough was or that the girls here were the prettiest in all of Ireland. (Which for most men is a better sell than a dozen sun-kissed beaches and a thousand shopping centres.)

And he shouldn't have been shot. He had teed off a lot of people with his early support for the new police, by wearing his bloody poppy and strong-arming the weak into letting him get his own way. But if you start shooting people for minor misdemeanours like those, you'd knock out three-quarters of the pan-nationalist front. No, Bent did what he felt was necessary at the time.

Politics is not a game for conscientious people. It is about getting your way at all costs. It is about winning. You have to be able to wipe out people who stand in your way – and preferably in a manner which stops them from ever standing in your way again.

In the old days, our methods of winning (and wiping people out) were, admittedly, quite crude – but they were effective. But we've supposedly stopped all that now and are in the business of learning real politics – craft, guile and deceit – as perfected by our Southern neighbours over the last century or so. And Bennett, for all his flaws, had learned well from them.

You and I, Sue, are too pretty for this game, I fear. Too innocent, even. There's been a lot of talk about me running in this by-election, but there's still some small shred of me that wants to remain pure. And I know that once I launch myself into that cesspit, I will not emerge smelling of roses. I will get as dirty as the rest – dirtier even, because I don't have it in me to lose.

And yet, I really don't want to become what Bent was. I don't want to become so despised that a neighbour can blow my head off my shoulders in broad daylight, in my own garden – and no one sees what happened, or even cares. I don't want the parish priest to have to pressurise some on-the-make contender into giving my lukewarm eulogy because no one else has two decent words to say about me. I don't want my widow (you) to read, two days after I die, that I was involved in so many shady land deals that even the gravediggers had to kickback 10 per cent to my estate. I don't want to be a byword for corruption, I don't want to be a running joke and I don't want to be a hypocrite.

I'm not going to run.

I love you always, Sue
Shay

Carsonville
Greencastle

Dear darling Shay

Settle yourself and stop worrying. You did well on Bennett. Very well. He was a man who had become rotten, not because he was innately evil, but because of his environs. He operated in a sewer – but, as you wisely pointed out, some people have to if the rest of us are to enjoy the benefit of clean water.

I understand entirely why you don't want to become him. But here's the thing – you won't. And I know you won't for two reasons – first, you worked out a long time ago that cheats, no matter how good they think they are, always get caught; and secondly, I would break every bone in your beautiful body if you let us down.

You have to run. No question about it. You're the only option. Caddle the Shinner has more dirty linen than a back-street knocking shop – and don't get me started on Deverry. He's even worse than you were with women, back in the day. I'd be afraid to leave him alone in a room with a medium to well-done fillet steak.

We all know that 99 per cent of why a politician runs for anything is ego – from village council to president of Ireland. It's not about wanting to help people, or making a difference, or governance or governing – or, heaven help us, the issues. (Do you believe some people actually buy that crap?) It's about vanity, pure and simple. You do it because there is no sweeter feeling than coming first in a race and then looking back down your nose at your inferiors.

But in your case, I would argue, it is not about ego – or exclusively about ego, at least. You genuinely have to go forward if only to stop the alternative. You cannot sit back and allow Tony Soprano's ugly cousin or some ass-groping time bomb become the premier representative to the world for your constituency – and, more importantly, for you. Even Fr Giddens would have to concede that in this particular race, you are the least of all evils.

The only real damage you could do is if you split the vote with either the Shinners or the Stoops (or both) and one of our lot slips in – somebody like Dexter Hart. And even then, I'm sure you'd be forgiven. Dex is one of the finest unionists never to hold high office, and most of your corner would vote for him in a flash if his grand-father hadn't been the local landlord (and hangman). But if you're ahead on the first opinion poll – which you will be – the Shinners and Stoops will be obliged to self-sacrifice for the greater good.

Have you also considered the possibility, Shay, that you're just scared? But what you have to remember is that you've nothing left to be scared of. All your skeletons are out there – and those damned lies about Ailis Kernanny died along with that bastard Bent.

I also appreciate you'll probably have to announce what you actually stand for – i.e. your national politics and your liaison with Dublin – and that this frightens you as well. But you have a better grasp of the broad view than anyone I've ever met. You have the rare gift of making decisions based on rationale, and then delivering on your promise via your charm. You can work a dancehall or barroom as well as the next parish-pump pol, but you're also fit to legislate and orate with the best Irish parliamentarians.

Give it a go, Shay. I want to watch my star rising.

I love you forever and forever
Sue

Memo: SG/BG

Brendy

Okay, it's time to batten down the hatches. I'll need to know the date of the by-election for Frank Bennett's seat – and also the date that nominations close. Could you also find out if there's any special nominating conditions? Oh, and I know you were hoping to head off in early January, but there might be a campaign. How are you fixed?

Shay

Memo: SG/Tommy Bowtie

Tommy

As you predicted, Sue's all for it as well. Wants to see her 'star rising', God love her wit. Personally, I'd much sooner stay put and leave it to someone else. Honestly. I'm not sure I want the hassle of London three days a week and the higher public profile (which in my case is a sure invitation to mockery, disaster and posthumous humiliation).

Nonetheless, it's very compelling when I hear both yourself and herself tell me that I'm the only one fit for this job – and that you think I really could make a difference.

People who say flattery doesn't work on them are liars. Of course it does. What we're really saying is that we're smart enough to work out that we're being flattered. But there's not one of us who can stop ourselves from sucking down the nectar. Our egos need nourished – every bit as much as our bellies. And when we're hungry enough and think nobody's looking, we suck down the honeyed words like a footballer's wife. For all that, Tommy, I'd remind both you and Sue that Danté consigned flatterers to the eighth circle of hell, where they reside forever in rivers of excrement (along with tabloid reporters and reality TV stars).

Anyway, we'll have a look at this thing. I'm making no promises, mind. I'm also reserving the right to pull out at any stage without you busting my hole about it. Despite whatever deal you think you struck with my uncle, I and I alone will be the final arbiter when it comes to my career. I already have a good job, good salary and good quality of life – in spite of the occasional flashback. And if there comes a point when it's too much, I will not be slow in letting you know.

You'll need to liaise with the SDLP as soon as possible to see if we can sort out a free run. Probably better I don't sit in on that meeting. The Stoops are still mad at me for making squeaking noises every time a certain high-pitched member of their front bench stands up to speak in the Assembly.

The Shinners, as you're aware, have changed their minds and don't want to put up a man this time – but they would probably feel obliged to if Deverry were nominated, if only to prove they can outpoll him.

Shay

PS Any thoughts on what I should buy Sue for Christmas? It's our last before we get married, so it has to be special.

PPS Did you know that politicians get to live out eternity in the eighth ring of hell as well? Apparently, we're all housed in a big vat of boiling tar – and demons with pitchforks torment any of us who try to get out. You'll not find that on the DUP manifesto.

Memo: BG/SG

Shay

As Bennett was an independent, the Scottish Nationalists moved the writ for the by-election in parliament yesterday. The dates are as follows: poll – 4 February; close of nominations – 16 January. The nominating conditions will be exactly as those for a normal Westminster election.

I'm afraid I take up my new job mid-January, so I'll not be about for the campaign. Raging about that. Would have loved to work for an MP. I'll have Grayson trained up fully before then. He'll handle it like a charm. Very smooth. Confidentially, maybe a bit too smooth? (Or is that just my jealousy?)

Regardless, you're going to win this thing by a country mile.

Brendy

PS And thanks again for the start-up gift. You shouldn't have. Be sure and thank Sue as well for me.

Memo: Tommy/SG

Shay

May I remind you that I am a double divorcee who sleeps on the office couch and hasn't had his relic rubbed since Paris Hilton was a good Catholic schoolgirl. Asking me for advice on what Christmas present to buy Sue is a bit like asking Bertie Ahern if he'd take a personal cheque. It can only end in tears.

Luckily for you, however, I am very well versed in what are *not* considered suitable as seasonal gifts. And I am more than happy to pass on the benefit of my extensive research. Consider this a service to both my gender and indeed humankind as a whole.
In my (very bitter) experience, there are ten prospective presents you should always stay away from.

Number 1 is, of course, lingerie. There are only three possible outcomes: (a) 'That's far too large, you must think I'm a big fat elephant.' (b) 'That's way too small, it'll make me look like a big fat elephant.' Or (c) 'I don't care if it is exactly my size, I'm not wearing anything with peepholes, you pervert.'

Number 2 is chocolates – seemingly innocuous, but in actual fact deadlier than a Russian tea party. Typical feminine riposte: 'What? Are you being funny? Do you not think I'm fat enough already?' (Just try it – there is no right answer to this question.)

Sticking with the sugary theme, and no-no Number 3 is body chocolate: 'You'll be lucky. I don't care what you cover them with, I'm still not licking them.' (Last time I'm shaving my armpits for anybody.)

Moving on to Number 4: champagne. Again, this is deceptively dangerous: 'Oh, I love bubbly. Thank you, so, so much. I'm going to drink it all by myself. Though sometimes it leaves me a little gassy . . .' (Trust me, this is NOT the sort of gas you want during foreplay.)

Number 5, and a favourite of rookies, is edible underwear. Suffice to say, the only time I tried it, I came home from work the next day to find my favourite silk boxers deep-fried and sitting in the middle of my dinner plate.

Number 6, and particularly perilous for the as yet unmarried, is emerald earrings: 'You just couldn't commit to putting them on a gold ring, could you?'

Number 7, and a sore one for me personally, a new pink Porsche with white leather seats and an idiot-proof sat-nav: 'Ooooh! That must have cost you a fortune . . . What's the matter? Did your other tart not want it, then?'

Number 8, a wrapped box containing an IOU for a back rub, foot rub and neck massage: 'A foot rub? Seriously. What are you, man? A pansy?'

Number 9, a teddy bear: 'Christ, what age do you think I am? Four? Where's my diamonds, you turd?'

And finally, and worst of all, Number 10 – flowers: 'Carnations!! Car-fucking-nations? You think I don't know they came from the garage? You spent more on the pack of condoms you bought from the same cashier . . . Typical. You couldn't be bothered to plan ahead and buy anything decent. So instead, you mean bastard, you hoped that a five-quid bouquet would get you the same sort of loving as a silk scarf, a three-course meal at La Trattoria and a moonlit carriage ride along the river. Well, I've got news for you, Mister, it doesn't. So take the flowers back to the garage, get a refund on your four pounds ninety-nine, and then buy yourself a fresh watermelon and a six-inch hole-punch. Because that's the nearest thing to any action you're going to get tonight [*Brutal face-slap*]. Now, go to hell!'

Hope this helps!
Tommy B

Dear Sue

Safe at home again following last night's pre-Christmas cabaret for MLAs up at Stormont. Sorry you couldn't be there. But as talent shows go, well, suffice to say that loud clang you can hear is the sound of Louis Walsh bolting the chamber door after him on his way out . . .

MC for the night was the Speaker, Willie Hay, on the grounds that if he was man enough to throw Iris Robinson out of the chamber, a couple of dozen oiled-up Provos would be no problem. Willie, of course, was accompanied with subtitles along the bottom of the stage, for those who live east of the Bann.

First up was the singing competition, which is normally a compulsory event for the four main parties. Ian Paisley Junior had been expected to feature strongly with a medley from *My Fair Lady*. But he withdrew at the last minute after the Free Ps' Heterosexual Ethics Committee refused to approve the lyrics of *Why Can't A Woman Be More Like A Man?* (And apparently Ian Óg has seen enough spotlights for one year anyway.)

No matter, the UUP leader Reg Empey kicked proceedings off with a highly convincing rendition of Status Quo's *Down, Down, Deeper And Down*. But he lost points for poor fretwork on his air guitar, and let's face it, he could never outperform some other notables in his party when it comes to head-banging.

Alex Maskey was up next for the Shinners with the Chucky ballad *Only Our Rivers Run Free* – but as he pointed out himself, they'll probably have to re-think the title whenever Peter Robinson introduces water charges.

Maskey indeed looked like he'd done enough to win the house vote. But that was before the Minister for Hard Calls Margaret Ritchie swooped in and stole the show with her version of the Barenaked Ladies anthem *If I Had A Million Dollars (. . . The UDA Wouldn't Get A Cent)*.

An honourable mention should also go to the group effort of David Ford (AP), Alex Attwood (SDLP) and Basil McCrea

(UUP) for their very credible rendering of *Stuck In The Middle With You*. 'Clowns to the left of me, jokers to the right . . .' – rarely were truer words ever spoken.

Next, you had the impersonation contest – an event in which the Shinners traditionally do very well. And Martin McGuinness gave an almost entirely realistic imitation of a man not at all irked by being repeatedly called Deputy. But the laurels this year went to the ex-DUP stalwart Jim Allister for his ceaseless and unending impression of Ian Paisley Senior – Ian Paisley pre-April 2007, that is.

The recitation section of the evening was also hotly contested, as you'd expect from a bunch of people who spend their lives learning off the party mantra. But it was the free-thinking SDLP stalwart John Dallat who took the crown, for his rousing interpretation of *If I Had The Wings Of A Sparrow*, which he dedicated to his former party colleague turned Shinner, Billy Leonard. Dallat, however, clearly thought he was back home on Radio Foyle and had to be carried off with a bag over his head after his fifth encore.

The night culminated in a heated round of the 'Yes! No!' game where if you answer any given question with either word you are gonged off the stage. Gregory Campbell was a particularly strong performer, baffling both the crowd and quizmaster alike with his ability to construct huge long sentences without conveying either answer – or indeed anything else remotely comprehensible.

Dawn Purvis also proved quite a skilled prevaricator, though she's had a lot of practice of late – every time she's called on to clarify if the UVF have decommissioned or not.

Unfortunately, however, someone thought it would be all right to allow the Sinn Féin MLAs Raymond McCartney and Gerry Kelly to play as well. And the two old IRA men wound up splitting first prize, after they both studiously ignored everything they were asked, picked a spot on the wall and stared at it, hard. The training never leaves you (allegedly).

The evening ended with a toast to the visiting dignitaries. But unlike previous gatherings, when members of the different communities would make a diplomatic exit before the other's national anthem, this time everyone slipped out together to avoid Phil Coulter's *Ireland's Call*.

See you at the weekend.

Love always
Shay

Owen Macha House
Mountain Brae Road
Dunavady

Dear Mr Gallagher

First of all, my congratulations on your fine oration at Frank Bennett's funeral. It was a statesman-like performance and redeemed the entire borough after it had been shamed by such a dastardly act.

I understand from this morning's *Standard* that you are considering allowing your name to go forward to replace Mr Bennett as our MP. I have been very impressed by the way you have conducted yourself as an impartial and independent Assemblyman at Stormont and wonder if you would consider allowing me to help you with your campaign?

As you are aware, I have previously been a public representative for Londonderry North (once polling 5,500 votes!), albeit representing a different community. But now I think, in the spirit of the new age, it would be most advantageous to the constituency as a whole if I were to throw my support, and indeed 'war chest', behind you.

I would very much like to meet you, at your earliest convenience, to discuss this further. My nephew, Grayson McKeepney, whom I was delighted to learn you have engaged as your new assistant, will furnish you with all my contact numbers.

Yours sincerely
Victor McLaughlin
Chief Executive, United Development Industries NI

Memo: SG/Tommy

Hi, Tommy

Letter from Switchblade Vic attached. Not sure I want to be too cosy with the likes of him. Time was, he'd have been wallowing up to his neck in my Fenian blood. But it'd knock Dexter Hart's challenge into the ditch for sure. What do you reckon?

Shay

PS Can you believe Serpico's his nephew? That apple fell so close it bounced right back up the fucking tree.

Memo: Tommy/SG

Shay

You're right to be careful about Vic. We could certainly do with his money, as you're ridiculously overspent again. But I think we both have a fair idea what he'll be looking for in return.

Three questions. One, do we need him to get you elected? Answer: probably not.
Two, would it be a useful political alliance? Answer: ultimately, he's a gangster, albeit an increasingly well-dressed one, so long term it'll do us more harm than good.
Three, would it be a profitable alliance? Answer: almost certainly. Extremely.

I think we should sit down and talk about this. Realistically, if there's going to be a Dunavady bypass, it might as well go through Vic's land on our watch than go through it when the next guy takes over.

The SDLP are just off the phone, by the way. It's just as I feared. They're not at all keen to move aside for you. They're dressing it up as being 'necessary for the democratic process', but you can sense the avarice in Deverry's voice. He wants the status, he wants the power – and he wants the expenses. I pointed out that he hadn't a pup's chance, but the idiot has convinced himself he's going to go through an entire campaign without someone leaking details of the four different sexual harassment suits still outstanding against him. I almost feel sorry for him.

Now, where's that file?
TB

PS The good thing about you spending eternity in the eighth ring of hell is that you'll never have any bother finding a lawyer.

Chief Superintendent's Office
PSNI, Derry

Hi, Shay

I've just received Serpico's notice – he tells me he's going to work for you. Have you taken leave of your senses, man? Has all the blood drained out of your brain and into those other organs you've spent the past twenty years overusing? Or has he, as I suspect, got the goods on you?

Please assure me, by return, that you intend to spend the next five years sleeping with a gun under your pillow. Seriously, this is a particularly devious article we're talking about – even for a cop. You know his family connection, I take it?

Well done on the graveside speech, by the way. You buried Caesar without unduly praising him. And I'll gladly sign the nomination papers, as before, if you wish. The Policing Board can whinge all they want, but I'm back off to the Guards in six months, so fuck them.

Ed

PS Run this letter through the shredder. Twice.

Carsonville
Greencastle

Dear Shay

I'm finding it a little hard to believe what's happening here. First you're blowing off Christmas dinner with us – because you've got to appear at three pensioners' functions in North Derry? And now you expect me to believe that Victor McLaughlin is joining your campaign on some cross-community kick? I hope you know what you're doing. If I didn't trust you with my life, I'd swear to God you were on the take. Be very careful of that man – beneath that cold, calculating façade lies the heart of a bad-minded bastard.

I know I was the one who suggested recruiting Serpico. And I still think it's a good idea. We all need watchdogs to protect us. We need people we can send into the world to do our dirty dealings, to hand out and receive brown envelopes and never tell us about them, to spin, to puncture, to wound, to kill and never let it rebound on their masters. Carlos Fuentes, the Mexican writer, says that corruption is the grease that oils the wheels of democracy. And the longer I'm at this, the more I believe him.

I like to think I myself have stayed relatively straight and, dare I say it, clean during my career to date. But I know I wouldn't have lasted five minutes if there weren't people at my elbow prepared to bury a few bodies for me. (Thank God for a live-in mother!)

You'll find, in particular, when you get to Westminster (note the 'when' – not 'if') that Serpico's talents as a hatchet man will be essential. Up in North Derry, you carry clout, no doubt about it. And you've also got some stock at Stormont. But over across the water, you'll be the fresh-faced kid in the new uniform, just ripe to be flushed down the big boys' toilet, unless you've someone watching your back.

For all that, you have no option but to contest the seat. It's essential you move on from pothole politics, if only for your own sanity. For all our grand titles, high salaries and insane expenses, we Stormont jocks are no more than a bunch of housewives divvying up whatever allowance the absentee husband gives us. At the very least, in London you'll be able to twist the fucker's arm for a few more bob.

Bitching session over – on to happier things. I'm thrilled, as is Danielle, that you're making it down for Boxing Day. And despite my carping, I know that, yes, sticking your neb into three OAP dinners is just the sort of thing that could give you the edge on 4 February. I'll wait and let you unwrap your Christmas stocking yourself. (Though we'll hold off till my mother goes out to her sister's. Otherwise, well, it would just be plain distasteful . . .)

I can't tell you how much I love the pearl-studded wristwatch. Just when I think you can't astound me with your brilliance any more, Shay, you go and leap the bar. They used to say down this part of the world that a watch was a 'parting gift' that a fella would give to a girl he's about to get shot of. But lucky me, I'm marrying you in less than eight months time. Wow! It takes my breath away.

I'll go now and post this so it doesn't get lost in the pre-Christmas rush. I love you and can't wait to see you next weekend for a good old-fashioned game of Christmas Cluedo. (Scarlet Lady in the Conservatory with the Handcuffs.)

Sue

PS I'm still intrigued as to how you put Deverry out of the game. I suppose it was Tommy? It smells of his sinister hand.

Memo: Ned Broy/Ailis Kernanny

Ailis

Call to the homestead anytime after four on Christmas Day – as soon as you can get away for your 'power-walk'. The earlier the better – it is Christmas, after all!

S

We had taken bets on how long it would take Victor McLaughlin to show his face after Bennett's murder. Shay felt he would wait at least a month for the sake of decorum – that he wouldn't want to appear greedy. But Vic had a neck like a kick-boxer's codpiece, and I knew he'd make his approach before Christmas.

I'm not sure Shay realised just how money hungry – and indeed dangerous – Vic was. Probably just as well, or he'd never have exposed himself to the hazards of a parliamentary election. My own measure for dealing with people like Vic has always been to imagine my own absolute bottom line, the line to which I would only ever stoop to save my own skin, and then remember that there are those who will crawl under even that. In saying that, I have to tip my hat to him for the skill he showed in getting his nephew into place.

At least with Vic you could see what was coming. Watching Shay's dealings with Ailis Kernanny was like waiting for the boom from a no-warning bomb. Even now, I get the shakes when I think of the number of times it could have blown up in our face.

JANUARY

Confidential Memo: Tommy/SG

Shay

Happy New Year, you fine thing, you – and many thanks for the case of Hennessy XO. You are the only man alive who loves me and appreciates me for what I am.

Good news! This time next year we'll be millionaires – at least, if Vic McLaughlin has his way we will. I got his first cheque this morning and I've processed it as we agreed. We have to be very careful how we handle this man. As I told you first day, he's not interested in you for your mind – or even your pretty body. It's about your influence – pure and simple. The only two things that money and power are ever concerned with are *more* money and *more* power. And with you, he's got access to both.

Fianna Fáil have agreed to pick up the tab for your leaflets, posters and other election paraphernalia. But they'd rather you didn't brag about it, as they govern their own country and are not, officially, supposed to get involved in Westminster elections. FF also don't want to jeopardise their petting session with the SDLP, and the Stoops, as you know, are still a bit sore about how I nobbled Deverry. For some reason, they expect us to have higher standards than the rest of the pack. Quaint, isn't it?

Talking of Deverry, from what I hear, his days as an MLA are numbered. Apparently, his PA has got tired of lying for him to all his other girlfriends and has blown the whistle. (If a girl could only stick to blowing whistles . . .)

Watch this space, as I think we're looking at a sudden resignation for family reasons. This is a very precarious business we're in, Shay. All it takes is one pebble to scoot out of the dam and we're up to our fucking necks in water. And as an MP, you're going to be subject to even closer scrutiny, so for Chrissake, remember the three golden rules I gave you when you started out:

1. Never write anything into a computer (or look at anything on a computer) that you couldn't produce in open court.
2. Keep all your business meetings one on one – that way there can be no witnesses.
3. Always assume that your every move is being filmed and your every word is being taped.

This is not paranoia; this is twenty-first-century politics. There are maybe two people in this world you can trust – me, because as your lawyer I can never testify against you, and Sue. But even with her, you're going to have to marry her first. If you reckon I'm laying it on too thick, just think back on what I myself have done to the last half-dozen or so people who tried to harm you.

The reason I'm reiterating all this now is twofold. One, that fucker Serpico is now in residence and I don't trust him an inch; and secondly, AK was spotted exiting The Eyrie on Christmas Day – by a friend, thank God. A good friend, who can keep his mouth shut. You can't be doing this, Shay. And anyway, it's no longer necessary. It's like the time you drove all the way into Derry to try out their new Park and Ride system – it can only end in disappointment.

If nothing else, consider the political consequences. The Shinners, as we gathered, aren't going to field a candidate against you – but there's still a week before nominations close, so you really must try not to piss anybody off. It looks like it's just going to be yourself and Dex, and with the built-in 55–45 split, it should be yours – unless, of course, you devise a way to fuck it all up.

So remember: head down, best behaviour, and leave the dirty stuff to me.

Tommy B

PS Run this memo through the shredder, like a good chap. This minute.

The Eyrie
Dunavady

My dearest Susan

I miss you terribly. This campaign is taking up far too much of my time. It was great to get down to Tyrone for the New Year, though. And much kudos on that new resolution you've adopted. (Good job you waited until we were engaged, or I'd never have had to marry you.)

Can I promise you now, as soon as this election is over, I'll never spend another holiday or weekend away from you. It's not worth it. Life is too short to spend it all in the fast lane. And I'm sick to the teeth with all this behind-the-scenes ducking, diving, skulduggery and chicanery. I often feel that you're the only good and decent thing left in my life. I sometimes wish I'd taken up an honourable calling, like drug-dealing or body-snatching.

You were wrong about Vic, though. His money is no dirtier or cleaner than anybody else's. And there's never been a minute's pressure from him about the bypass. His only stipulation has been that I don't remove it from the political agenda entirely. Which is fair enough. As you know, I've always had an open mind regarding the development. And now Bennett's route (which was every bit as twisted and misdirected as he was) has been ruled out, I think we can start afresh and look at new ideas.

Even Tommy reckons the Commons seat will be mine now – barring, of course, events, dear girl, events. But there's no way you'll hear anyone saying that out loud, as we're all far too long in this business to go baring our arses to Fate. Nonetheless, for the first time, I'm starting to think about the possibilities of the role – particularly within the context of the new all-Ireland dispensation. For the first time ever, Northern MPs have speaking rights in the Dáil. And while you and I know this carries about as much weight as leering rights at a strip show, there's always the possibility we can, ah, lap up some extras.

The problem with the South at the moment is that for the first time in almost two decades there's a fear sneaking back into the economy. They're so worried about losing their new-found wealth that they're cutting back on everything. And they certainly won't want to waste their savings on a prospect as volatile and as thankless as the North.

I hate to sound dismal, but I do fear for this place in the long term. The war here – like most wars – was about inequality. It's the first rule of teaching – every child should be entitled to an equal share. And when everyone has their allocation, then everyone can be happy – or at least should have no right to complain. People tend to fight less with those who are poorer than them (unless they live in Iraq and we want their oil).

But given that we've got equality, of a sort, our constituents are soon going to realise that the prospects for both communities are equally bad. Now that the focus is off their own petty squabbles, they are going to discover just how hard it is to compete in a world where plasma TVs can be produced for a tenner apiece in China and where call-centre workers in India will do the job for a fifth of what people are paid here. And our Get Out of Jail card, which was effectively 'Give us extra or we'll blow up your Stock Exchange', is no longer valid. The question for our new masters is: will we still all be happy to sing off the same hymn sheet when the collection boxes are empty?

If I sound gloomy, it's only because I'm a little under pressure with all the extra work. Thank Christ for Serpico; he's like Brendy but better organised. You were right. He is exactly what I needed. The only calls he ever puts through directly to me are yourself and Tommy B – everyone else is screened. And unlike Brendy, he reads situations very quickly, without needing things spelled out. Oh, and he's brilliant, just brilliant, with the press. He knows exactly who to stroke, who to cajole and who to threaten. (And because of who he is, and where he's been, his threats tend to carry a great deal more weight than mine or yours.)

One final thing – can you tell Danielle I absolutely loved her present? Seriously. I actually choked up when I opened it – though don't tell her that, or she'll be figuring me for a big pushover. I'm drinking my late-night cuppa out of it now – World's Greatest Dad.

Jesus, she knows how to tweak my strings. Just like her mother.

I love you always, my princess
Shay

Memo: G/V

Uncle Vic

We own him!

It didn't take me two minutes to get into his personal safe – tip for beginners, never use your date of birth as a security code. For a pro like myself, it's just far too easy – yet about one in three people use some variant of their DoB (or their partner's) to protect their most intimate and valuable belongings. They should have their arses kicked every half-hour for thirty minutes, as McKenna would say.

Shay's weakness is that he's a sentimentalist and can throw nothing out. He tried to convince me that Tommy has it drilled into him to destroy all personal correspondence. But I knew fine well that he would never shred any letter he'd received from Sexy Susie. And sure enough, they were all there in the safe – five years' worth.

What I hadn't counted on was that he'd keep copies of all the letters he sent to her as well. What an amateur. And it's here we struck gold. Because just three days before a certain MP was showered all over his rose garden, our Mr Gallagher was threatening to provide some hard men with the plans to that same MP's house and grounds. Threatening in pen and ink, that is. The prat. And I thought cops had no brains. He'd nothing to do with the hit, as you well know. But that doesn't matter.

Anyhow, a copy of the unfortunate letter is attached – which you can tell him you got from an anonymous MI5 man who works in the Post Office's little back room. He'll not suspect me. He hasn't got the guile.

There's enough in what he wrote to keep him our bitch until we catch him with AK – which should only take another week or so. He's convinced the heat's off because I'm now on his side. All the electronic equipment is set up. There are three different pinhole spycams in his office already – one looking right out at him from his computer. I'm able to track every word he types into his machine – or handwrites on the pad on his desk. (He picks his nose an awful lot, the dirty git – he's going to give himself polyps.) Thirty-five pounds per camera and less than an hour to set the three of them up – if people knew how easy surveillance was, they'd never use the bathroom.

As we discussed last night, you absolutely have to get Gallagher to make a commitment to the bypass *before* the election. If it's a campaign pledge, it drastically reduces the chances of another damned inquiry after the fact. It might lose him a few republican votes, but with a ten-point gap, it'll not be a deciding factor – particularly since none of the hardliners are going to vote for the opposition anyway. Talking of which, Dexter Hart was very grateful for your most generous cheque and isn't at all annoyed that you're using him as your fallback option. 'Pragmatic politics' is how he termed it. I can think of better ways you could have spent that 20K, but I suppose there's no point in keeping a spare wheel if it's not pumped up.

G

Memo: GM/SG

Shay

Victor McLaughlin would like to set up a private meeting with yourself at your earliest convenience. It's about a confidential matter, so he says it's perfectly all right if Mr McGinlay can't make it. (Between ourselves, I don't think he wants him in on it.)

Serpico

Memo: SG/GM

Serp

Tell Vic tonight is fine – Tommy's away in Derry on business anyway.

S

Private Memo: SG/TB

Tommy

Shit, shit, shit! I'm in bother. That dirty cutthroat bastard Vic McLaughlin has something on me and wants to see me this evening. Call in first thing tomorrow. Please.

S

PS Destroy this immediately.

Memo: Tommy/SG

Shay

You stupid fuckwit. Handwritten notes only from this point on – until I tell you otherwise. Promise him nothing tonight. Let him know I'm running the show and you have to refer everything to me.

He's going to want a public statement on his bypass – and I can't see how you're going to avoid giving him it. I'm so angry with you right now, I honestly might just walk away. But it's not me you have to worry about. What the blazes do you think Sue's going to say?

T

Shay

Tomorrow's lead story as attached.

You owe me a big one. Anybody but you pulling a stunt like that and I would have skewered them a new hole. And the only reason I'm not going for you is that I know full well Dexter Hart is taking that fucker's blood money as well. And there's no way I'm going to be responsible for getting Hart elected – even if we have to suffer you, you prick.

It might seem unusual for a newspaperman to be getting up on his high horse like this, Shay, but for one of the few times in my life, I'm seriously fucking disappointed. I thought better of you. I thought I knew you.

Just so you know, I don't think you're doing this voluntarily; I'd be pretty certain Vic has you by the Orange halls. But you're letting us all down, regardless – and if I get a sniff of dirty money, I promise you sincerely, I'll have you thrown in jail.

And by the way, I'll not be at the Castle on Thursday night – nor indeed any other Thursday night.

Stan Stevenson

BYPASS COULD NOW BE A GOER – GALLAGHER

In a dramatic turnaround, the independent MLA Shay Gallagher last night said a "properly thought-out" bypass system could be a "boon" to Dunavady.

Mr Gallagher – who is the only nationalist candidate for the vacant North Derry seat at Westminster – said he had reconsidered his position at the behest of local business interests.

"A bypass, as long as it includes a direct through-road into our industrial estate, would dramatically improve our local infrastructure and the speed of our link to both Belfast and Dublin," he said.

"The problem with the previously proposed route was its failure to integrate with the town's existing traffic system. A route over the other side of the mountain – such as that suggested by United Development Industries NI – could in the right circumstances have some potential."

In another surprise move, the Ulster Unionist candidate Dexter Hart MLA said he had studied the latest consultancy reports and agreed entirely with Gallagher's plan. So it now looks certain the road will be developed.

But the anti-agreement unionist Fulcroom Lydock, who is also contesting the election, accused both men of being "inappropriately influenced" by commercial interests.

He told the Standard: "The new road is going to go through land owned almost exclusively by Victor McLaughlin, a major sponsor of the Gallagher campaign and a friend of Hart to boot.

"I have spoken to the Chamber of Commerce and they are appalled at this volte-face by these two lackeys. Switchblade Vic has scored himself another large slice of pie – but the rest of us are going to pay for it for all eternity.

"This town could lose ten million pounds a year in passing trade – not to mention the industrial jobs that are going to head to Londonderry as soon as we're off the map."

The latest polls show Gallagher will take the seat comfortably. He is sitting at 56 per cent, Hart is at 39 per cent while Lydock has 5 per cent.

Carsonville
Greencastle

Dear Shay

I want so much to be angry with you, but try as I might, I can't get past despair. I couldn't be more heartbroken if I'd found out you were seeing another woman. You might as well be, such is the betrayal. It's like the light has gone out inside me. I don't think I've ever felt so sad – not when Grandpa died, or even when I thought I'd lost Danielle.

Beneath your cynicism, Shay, I always knew you to be honest and decent. You always did the right thing – even if it meant putting yourself in danger. But now I'm seeing a side of you that I cannot accept – and will not live with. I truly believed that you were one man who, behind his cynical façade, would never corrupt himself. I was wrong.

The fact that you shut me out of your decision to do business with a man who spent thirty years killing and robbing people (and who, let's be honest, will still do so at the drop of a hat) speaks loudly to the future of our relationship. We no longer have any.

We have spent the past five years discussing everything, from my daughter's depressions, to your ambitions, to the wallpaper in our new house. A house that I now will never live in. But someone was finally able to pay the price you needed to allow your true colours to emerge – and walk away from me – and you took it.

I never figured you were harbouring a cowardly streak– but it's been two days since the newspaper reports and you still haven't called me. What is it you're afraid of? Looking in the mirror?

For the first time in my life, Shay, I feel truly defeated. There is no longer anything good in my world. And you, and you alone, have made me feel that way. The last five years have been a con. You have played me for a naive fool – and now you've won. Saddest of all, I'm too empty even to resent you for it. I've nothing left inside of me.

I thought we had all this love – right up to the moon and back

94

– and now, out of nowhere, it's gone. Where the hell did it go, Shay? Where the hell did *you* go?

Susan

The Eyrie
Dunavady

Dear Susan

I cannot believe you would turn on me like this – without so much as a right of reply. It must be lonely for you, on your own, up there on the moral high ground. Seriously, lady, where do you get off?

If politicians were restricted to doing business with people who had clean hands, there'd be nobody left at Stormont but the Alliance Party swapping knitting patterns with the Women's Coalition. Our two sectarian factions spent thirty years not talking to one another because we both considered the other too dirty, and look how far that got us.

I'm afraid I don't do guilt, princess – not about practicalities at least. You think I'm crooked because I change my mind? And then you compare this to me cheating on you? I'm just doing my job, same as yourself, trying to make life better for my neighbours – something I've been doing since the day we first met. Sometimes it's not pretty; fair enough, but at least it gets done. And it's nothing more, or nothing less, than what you yourself do everyday. So it's a bit late to be hitching up your skirts now, sister.

Just for the record, I would never have betrayed you, Sue. It's not in me. You are the one absolute in my life. Or rather, you were. But I think you're right about us not knowing one another. I never figured you for sanctimonious. And if you're too empty to be angry, rest assured, I'm not.

I'll tell you where our love went – it got drowned in a big vat of self-righteous bullshit. I'll get Tommy to sort out the house with you. Don't worry, you'll get everything you're owed.

Shay

Memo: SG/GM

Hi, Serp

Could you take this envelope down the street to my friend with the bow tie. For fuck's sake don't drop it – or lose it. You know the score yourself.

Shay

Eyes Only: SG/TB

Tommy

Just fucked up again and broke Rule Whatever-Number in your book – never write anything down in a temper. Short version, you'll be getting a call from Sue. Please, please don't do anything with the house just yet.

Shay

Memo: G/V

Uncle Vic

He went on the offensive with the letter to her as I advised him. (I'm now his confidant on top of everything – how paradoxical is that?) I'm pretty certain he's burnt all his bridges. Pity. She's a lovely girl – just too darned straight.

I still think we should throw a scare into Shay with the Kernanny stuff, just to be doubly sure. We haven't quite got enough to use – a few pictures of her leaving his house is the height of it. But he doesn't know that. The threat alone will put the fear of God in him. We wouldn't even have to say we were going public with them – only that we'll show them to Dead-Eye Daithi and allow him to make up his own mind. That'd stall any thoughts Shay might have of running to the media to purge his guilt over the Bennett killing.

Talking of which, he's also fallen out with Stan Stevenson of the *Standard*. Stan's gone and got himself a dose of the holier-than-thous over Shay's link-up with yourself. He's even threatening Shay with bad press. You might want to lean on our esteemed editor and remind him that he's not above the law either – not as long as you still have that tape of him asking you to set fire to his old offices. Is there anything in life as satisfying as debunking a hypocrite?

G

Carsonville
Greencastle

Shay, you wastrel bastard. You broke more than my mother's heart. I'm no innocent. I'm nearly fifteen years old and stopped believing in Santa long ago, but I always thought I could spot the good guys from the bad ones. But fair play to you, you fooled me. Granny, too. She actually held my mother's hand and cried along with her.

Mum's not going to come out of this one. Not the full way. I can see the bitterness setting into her face. Despite everything she's gone through in her life up till now, she always remained soft – trusting, even. But you've hardened her, Shay; you've shut off the light; and for that, I will never forgive you.

I'm returning your typically extravagant Christmas cheque, now I know where the money came from – and my key to the new house. I would be grateful if you would take the little token I gave you and smash it against your kitchen wall. Not even you could be such a hypocrite as to hold on to it.

Just so you know, anything bad that happens to your car, flat or person over the next few months, you can safely assume I did it. Like yourself, I've chosen to be angry about this. Only, my anger is justified.

Danielle McEwan

Memo: Tommy/SG

Shay

Want to hear something hilarious? Vic has asked for his cheque back. I suppose he's worked out he doesn't have to pay you any more. Bad enough he caught you with your 'I'll kill Frank Bennett' letter, he's now telling me he has pictures of you and AK. Oh, joy of joys! You're going to spend the rest of your days as his arse-wiper-in-chief.

May I recommend, as perhaps the only person still speaking to you, that you withdraw from the election immediately and salvage a little dignity?

T

Memo: SG/GM

Serp

Could you do the needful with this envelope to our friend down the street? Thanks for your advice on the other matter. You're dead right – winners never quit.

Shay

Eyes Only: SG/TB

Tommy

So Vic gets his road, what harm? I'm a big boy and he caught me – but there's no reason to squander the opportunity of a lifetime just because one businessman has a little leverage. If you can tell me of one other politician who hasn't had to change his position occasionally, I'll throw in the towel right now. Vic is never going to embarrass me publicly, not so long as I've Serp around. The nephew is a strong moderating influence on Vic and is an expert at protecting my back – even from his uncle.

There are many other Victor McLaughlins out there hoping to do business with their new MP, and it would be a shame for you and me to let them down. You get one big chance in life, Tommy. This is ours.

S

Owen Macha House
Dunavady

Dear Mr Gallagher

I would like to thank you fulsomely for your recent statements endorsing the new bypass plan. Unfortunately, as you are already aware from my discussions with Mr McGinlay, I believe, for the sake of propriety, that I should confine my (unwavering) support for your election campaign to an advisory role. Any financial input from me at this stage could be misconstrued.

I would like to meet with you at your earliest convenience to assure you of my loyalty – and also to discuss the matter of secondary-school entrance criteria, which is troubling many of our friends across Ulster.

Yours sincerely
Victor McLaughlin
Chief Executive, United Development Industries NI

Confidential Memo: Tommy/SG

Shay

I met Susan this morning as you asked. And I now know for certain there is no God – as He could never have fashioned a soulless bastard like you in his image. Politics, as you will learn when you die alone, is only a job. The real world is what's important. You have made the cardinal error of confusing the two and now have no life at all.

Rest assured, though, your nest egg is safe. Sue's not looking for anything she's not entitled to. I cut her a cheque for what she'd put into the house plus another twenty grand appreciation, which you are giving her out of your own pocket. Any problems you might have with that, you can shove up your arse with our friendship.

She was wondering whether to make a public statement about your break-up, to stop the gossip going about. But I advised her not to. She's publicly gifting the Hart campaign a thousand pounds, which I think is statement enough. Plus she's going to come up here to canvass for him. It's just a shame she's too decent to stick a fucking knife in you while she's at it.

(When this campaign is over, by the way, if you hadn't already twigged, I'm gone as your agent. As for that business with Ailis Kernanny, you do know that the whole town is talking? You have precisely one week to shut that down before I tell her husband.)

You were asking me on the phone about the school boundaries' issue Vic is hassling you on. I'm not sure he's too bothered about it, to tell you the truth – other than to remind you that you are now merely the good-looking boy at the front of his shop. This is the first, I'm certain, of a hundred favours you're going to do for him, before the Jack Daniels dissolves his liver and that sinister fucker Serpico takes over. Anyway, the 'nearest-the-school' entrance criterion is annoying some of Vic's rich pals, who want to live out in the suburbs, or over the border, and then send their children to the finest academies in the city centres. Vic is now asking you – sorry, TELLING you

– to do away with catchment areas and instead allow the middle classes and the upper-middle classes first pick of the plum schools. Your best way to spin it is to pretend, like the Shinners, that the education system is discriminating against people living in the Free State – and that it's outrageous that innocent children should be precluded from attending a school in Derry, say, just because they live in Donegal. Make a virtue out of your republicanism – I'm sure it'll get you a few more votes. And never mind the working-class scum who live three streets away from the school are being done out of their rightful places.

Anyhow, before you do anything else, Shay, I'd highly recommend you first go out and buy yourself a big gallon jar of Vaseline. You're going to need it over the next five years.

Go to hell, fuckwit.

Tommy

PS I'm dropping this note off at The Eyrie myself, as I'm convinced Serpico is reading our memos. Don't send him down to my office anymore. Come down yourself.

Memo: G/V

Uncle Vic

You were right to be careful with McGinlay. He's a lot sharper than our man. Thank the Lord he's going to be off the scene. Shay is a lot more manageable himself alone. The last thing we want is to be dealing with another clever clogs. Please God, we'll not have to fertilise the roses with him like we did Frank Bennett.

McGinlay, the cute article, thought he'd drop a confidential letter into Gallagher's hacienda last night. But I caught him, thanks to our camera hidden in the gatepost, and got a quick copy of the note before Shay got back from the Credit Union AGM. (Find enclosed.)

Gallagher actually gave me my own key to the house, bless him. The alarm kept going off while he was at Stormont, so he gave me his duplicate – plus the alarm codes. (His date of birth – again!)

He's currently up in Belfast for the day, so I have the office to myself. The lunatics tend not to call in if he's not about. They know I'm too strict a gatekeeper. To keep myself entertained, I might replace the mike in his desk phone, as it's echoing a bit on the tape.

See you at church.

G

Memo: Ned Broy/AK

Ailis

The rumours are getting out of hand. Think it's time you told big D. I'm happy to come along if it'll help things. It's your call.

Say a prayer for me.

S

Parochial House
Dunavady

Dear Shay

I'm writing to you as a courtesy to alert you to a letter I have sent to the *Derry Standard* in reply to your latest missive on schools' criteria.

Your attack on our enrolment procedures at St Fiachra's

College was unspeakably unfair – so unfair that for the first time in my adult life I feel obliged to spoil my ballot on polling day. We do not, and have never, favoured middle-class children, as you, a former teacher of this college, know full well.

Your supporters have allowed you one major mistake, in the form of your U-turn over the bypass, but this nonsense now, coupled with the way you treated Miss McEwan, raises serious doubts about your suitability as our representative in parliament.

I know for certain that I am worth 2,000 votes to you in this election – Victor McLaughlin will not win you a single one. Be very careful, Shay, as you're not past the winning post yet.

Yours sincerely
Monsignor N Giddens DD

The Eyrie
Dunavady

Dear Susan

Please don't rip this up – but just recognise it for what it is, an abject apology.

The life went out of me when I met you on the canvass today. All my enthusiasm, determination and will to win just evaporated in an instant when I saw your face. You looked so broken, and I did that to you. I am truly, eternally sorry.

I don't expect you ever to forgive me, but I just want you to know that none of this was your fault. You made a bad choice in me. Or rather, I misled you – the most wonderful angel on this earth – into making a bad choice.

You don't have to worry, by the way, about me now pursuing you and then destroying you a second time; not even I could be that cold and heartless. For a short while, I truly believed that I could live up to the image I was projecting to you, but ultimately, I was always going to fail. And the only satisfaction

I can derive is that I failed before you married me and disgraced yourself entirely.

I intend to continue with this pointless political campaign as, to be frank, I have nothing else left in my life. That emptiness you spoke of before, well, I recognise it all too well now and need something to fill the hole. Tommy has all but cut me off, Father Giddens isn't speaking to me at all, and my only friend is a cunning and ruthless ex-cop I brought in to stop him spying on me. Though in fairness to Serp, I have never met a more dependable aide. He's the one thing stopping me from doing myself serious harm.

I'm a little drunk now as I write this. To be honest, I'm a little drunk now a lot of the time. But, as you always said, each of us uses what he needs to get by. The good news, from your part, is that my MI5 friend Jack White reckons the dissidents could take me out in their next surge. Truth is, they'd only be doing me a favour.

It's only ten days to polling day, so I suppose I should really go and lick some envelopes. I'll start with this one.

Forever ashamed
Shay

Read and Shred: V/G

Grayson

Thanks for flagging up the Kernanny situation – and very well spotted. We need to make sure Shay doesn't start acting on his conscience. It'd seriously weaken our grip on him – and might even blow the election.

I don't believe for one minute that Tommy Bowtie will really rat out his friend (and client) to the IRA's top marksman. Shay'd wind up dead as old buttons. But we have to be absolutely 100 per cent certain that Tommy says nothing – if you follow my drift. And if Tommy's not talking, well, I strongly doubt that Shay will feel the need to either.

Only problem is that if what Tommy is saying *is* true, we've only got a couple of days to stall him – three days at most. So, you would probably be best using the same machinery and same pattern you employed the last time. That'll make the post-game analysis all the easier for the likes of Jack White afterwards. He's already spent half the winter chasing dissident shadows – he may as well spend the spring doing likewise. We'll phone in a claim to say it was a warning to Gallagher not to sit on policing boards.

It should work out okay for Shay as well, in that he'll get to do his second public eulogy in a couple of months – and in election week, too. Not that he needs it, though. Despite all the scandal, dirt and allegations, he's still 12 per cent ahead.

Ditching Sue McEwan was worth a clear five points to him, no doubt about it. Every unattached woman under fifty in the borough now thinks she's got a shot at the title.

We'll just have to keep a tight watch to ensure he never reverts to his bachelor days. Though he's clearly starting to learn who's boss. By the end of the year, we'll have him wearing his poppy with pride – just like the late, lamented Francis did last year. Poor Frank, he thought he was teaching me a lesson with his Vady Construction proposal – pupil outsmarting the master and all that. But he forgot the golden rule, G, the rule that I've been drilling into you since day one: never, ever forget that there is always someone smarter than you in the game.

That's what stops you being careless.

V.

PS You'll find the 'appliances' in the same place.

Main Street, Dunavady

To: Stan Stevenson
Editor, Derry Standard, Dunavady

FOR IMMEDIATE PUBLICATION

Dear Editor

How your standards are slipping. A week before an election, you allow my opponent Fulcroom Lydock, a hardline unionist, to level a charge of corruption against me without giving me right of reply. This speaks volumes about your paper – a paper, incidentally, that parades itself as the 'nationalist voice' in Dunavady. It was almost as if you waited until the last minute to maximise the potential embarrassment to me.

Mr Lydock's allegations are patently false, as one phone call to me, or my lawyer Thomas McGinlay, would have established. There is no evidence whatsoever that I, at any stage, banked a cheque given to me by Mr McLaughlin or that I interceded improperly on his behalf regarding the bypass. I merely pointed out that there were two sides to the mountain – and that the road could equally well go along either side. I attach my original statement on the matter for your perusal.

Your additional claim that my former fiancée Susan McEwan ended our relationship because of my dealings with Mr McLaughlin was equally fallacious – and an extremely hurtful personal attack. One phone call to Miss McEwan would have established this – but again, it is a call you refused to make.

Mr McGinlay has already spoken to you about the terms of the front-page apology I understand you are going to publish today – and the considerable damages which you will present on my behalf to charity.

As the man who hopes to serve as the next MP for this area, it is not my wish to spend my term in constant conflict with the local press. But I will not tolerate such blatant and damaging lies about my character.

Yours
Shay Gallagher, MLA

Confidential Memo: SG/TB

Tommy

Would it be possible to meet you tonight to discuss the AK situation? We're going to tell Daithi tomorrow. Might be best for you and me to hook up somewhere totally out of the way. How about the car park at Ness Woods at about eight? I could be a couple of minutes late, as I've a young farmers' meeting in Drumbridge.

Shay

To: Chief Superintendent's Office
PSNI, Derry

Dear Ed

Our mutual friend Jack, who looks like a plumber, has been warning me of possible difficulties with my, ah, pipes – imminent difficulties, that is. Any chance you could spare me a few welders? Four would be best. It's either that or I could be left with several holes that might never be patchable. Sooner the better, too. Tomorrow, even, if possible – as I've a notion the solder is about to hit the fan.

Yours
Shay

Memo: G/V

Vic

A man has to be quick on his feet round here. Our boy popped out to go to the shop an hour ago, and I spotted him slipping into Bowtie's office with what looked like a note in his hand. I ran back the office tape and caught him penning a sneaky little memo. And you'll never guess what – the dirty dogs are going to move on the

AK situation tomorrow. They're going to cry blackmail. I think we may have a perfect opportunity to stop them tonight, though.

G

To: Chris Caddle
Sinn Féin Office
Lower Main Street
Dunavady

Chris, a chara

I just want to confirm the meeting for my office, tomorrow at 3.00 pm. It'll just be yourself, myself, Ailis and Daithi. Daithi has no idea what's coming, so wear a vest.

Le meas

Shay

Memo: SG/GM

Hi, Serp

I wonder if you could set up a meeting with Victor McLaughlin for tomorrow at 4.00 pm. Ask him to come in here if possible, as there's someone I'd like him to meet. I've been made aware of a tremendous business opportunity, which could prove lucrative for the borough and indeed local interests, but need advice on how best to handle the logistics. (And by lucrative, by the way, I mean revoltingly lucrative.)

Thanks again for your support and counsel recently. I couldn't have got through this difficult time without you.

Shay

To: Stan Stevenson
Derry Standard
Dunavady

Dear Stan

I'll be making a pretty important announcement tomorrow about 5.00 pm relating to my campaign. Tommy will ring you later this evening with the details, but it'll probably be worth saving a little space on the following day's front page.

Thanks for the apology, by the way. It was more gracious than we could have ever expected. But I suppose the picture looks entirely different when you are clued into the real facts. As a reciprocal gesture, we're more than happy now to forgo those cheques to charity.

Let's hook up tomorrow night for a drink after the paper's put to bed. I've missed our chats.

Yours

Shay

Memo: GM/SG

Shay

Any chance I could get off a couple of hours early this evening? I've a bit of personal business to take care of. My young nephew has a five-a-side match down in Toberleggy, and he's been on at me for months to go and see him play. I promise to make up the time.

Serp

PS Spoke to Uncle Victor and he'll be here at four tomorrow, come hell or high water. He sounded very excited.

To: Carsonville
Greencastle

Dear Sue

It's on. Just in case things don't work out, remember, I love you dearly – always did and always will. Tell Danielle many thanks for her letter. I appreciate her candour!

Forever yours
Shay

From: shay.gallagher@freedunavady.com
To: jack.white@nisecserv.com

Jack

Serp has just left. This better work.

Shay

I'm sure you'd worked it out long ago, dear reader. There was no way we were going to let Vic and Serpico waltz in the door and then walk right out again with the farm. Sure, 90 per cent of Shay's correspondence was true – it had to be for us to convince them. But as for the other 10 per cent? Now read on.

FEBRUARY

Hi, Shay

Attached is a preview copy of tomorrow's front page. Fair play to you, son. You had us all going. I'm buying tonight. I should never have doubted you.

Your friend
Stan

TOP LOYALIST ARRESTED FOR MP'S MURDER

The chairman of United Development Industries NI, Victor McLaughlin, is to be charged later this week with the murder of North Derry MP Francis Bennett.

Security sources say that McLaughlin – known to his associates as "Switchblade Vic" – made taped admissions as to his involvement in the throes of a joint PSNI/MI5 sting operation.

He was arrested yesterday at the offices of Dunavady Assemblyman Shay Gallagher, shortly after attempting to shoot dead the independent MLA.

Mr Gallagher, who played a key role in the covert operation to trap McLaughlin, is understood to have elicited the loyalist's confession – at which stage, four policemen who had been lying in wait, moved in to arrest the would-be killer.

Witnesses say that McLaughlin then pulled out a licensed pistol and fired at Mr Gallagher – but apparently the weapon malfunctioned, and it exploded in the gunman's right hand, tearing off his thumb and three fingers. He is currently under guard in Dunavady Hospital, where a special court will be called to session later today.

Derry police chief Ed

CONTINUED...

O'Conway told the Standard that McLaughlin will face further counts of extortion, money laundering, threats to kill and attempting to blackmail two public representatives, namely Shay Gallagher and Dexter Hart. It is understood both MLAs have handed over uncashed cheques to the police, signed by McLaughlin, which they were given as bribes to copper-fasten their support for a road development on McLaughlin's land.

Supt. O'Conway commented: "We are pleased to say we have now concluded the biggest anti-racketeering operation ever undertaken in North Derry. It was instigated following complaints of corruption involving the late Francis Bennett, who, we will show, had a very close and unhealthy financial relationship with Victor McLaughlin.

"We would like to thank both Shay Gallagher and Dexter Hart for their co-operation, and also the Tyrone MLA Susan McEwan, who has been working with us since the planning stages."

The police have refused to confirm that Bennett and McLaughlin clashed when the late MP demanded a substantial "finder's fee" before a vesting order would be issued to purchase McLaughlin's land for the Dunavady bypass. The shady deal could have made both men multi-millionaires. But McLaughlin is said to have grown tired of the partnership and ordered Bennett's killing.

The PSNI last night removed a number of hidden cameras and listening devices which had been monitoring Shay Gallagher's office. Mr Gallagher confirmed that several of the cameras had been in position for more than a month and that he had been aware of their presence.

In a separate development, McLaughlin's nephew, Grayson McKeepney, who worked as an assistant in Mr Gallagher's office, has been reported missing. Police are very anxious to interview Mr McKeepney – but are also said to be concerned about his personal safety.

(See also Page 2: FF in mayoral talks with Sinn Féin – EXCLUSIVE)

Shay, a chara

I have to say Ailis wasn't wild when she worked out you'd been using her as a dupe over the past couple of months, but I'm sure the deal we struck yesterday will keep her sweet.

Daithi, as you anticipated, was a little reluctant at her becoming mayor – particularly given his past profile. But we took him out last night and explained to him, over copious bottles of stout, that I would do the bulk of the work of 'First Gentleman', so he settled down considerably. He was also somewhat mollified by the fact that I myself had sat in on each and every meeting relating to the mayoralty – including the one in your house on Christmas Day. Very clever, that, getting the picture of the two of you coming out of your pad together by convincing me to leave by the back door. I'd say when Serpico saw it, he must have thought he'd won the lottery. Next time, you fucker, clue me in!

We appreciate your support in next week's vote – especially as it should really be your turn in the chair, Shay. But you're right, we can't allow Fulcroom Lydock a turn; he'd embarrass the shit out of the borough. And besides, you can't do it, as you're going to have more than enough on your hands with your new job across the water. Who knows, I might even vote for you myself.

Slán go fóill
Chris Caddle MLA

Memo: SG/TB

Hi, Tommy

I think it's finally safe for me to write to you again without worrying about the camera over my desk or the one inside my computer monitor. That was one sharp idea of yours, by the way, to leave Vic's equipment in place and get Jack to add in a couple of our own to track Serpico. A classic double bluff from the master, and yet another reason why I never play poker with you. What is it Vic always says? Oh yes – never, ever forget that there is always someone smarter than you in the game. He should have it tattooed on his hairy knuckles. (Or, should I say, what remains of them . . .)

Your memos castigating me were quite brilliantly poisonous – some of them really stung. Though I did get a sense you were perhaps enjoying it a little too much. I think, however, you'll have to share the Booker Prize for Fiction with Sue, whose portrayal of a scorned and jettisoned lover was pitch perfect. And Dani will have to get a special mention in the Teen Literature Category for her furious denunciation of the evil villain what wronged poor maw. But again, I felt a couple of her threats were a little close to the bone. Were you, perhaps, helping?

A few things still need settling. Father G is quite clearly narked we didn't bring him in. I met him at the polling station and he looked about as happy as Papa Doc Paisley did when he was handed his goodbye note. (Who's chuckling now, buddy?) But we needed old Giddens to attack me publicly over the school boundary issue – and make it look real. I'll drop him a note this evening and attach it to something bottle-shaped, which might help.

I hope the irritable bowel has quietened. Like yourself, I found it a terrifying experience staring down the wrong end of a gun, waiting for it to blow up. It was tragic what happened to poor Serp, but it was his own doing. He'd that shotgun twenty-four inches from your forehead and wasn't shooting to wound.

Thank God for Jack White. But no matter how many times he told me he'd sealed up the barrels, the thought was always running through my head that the bullet would blast through the blockage and knock out my lights. I can only imagine your own case was even worse – even if it did end up like something out of a Daffy Duck cartoon. I've just heard on the wireless, by the way, that the cops finally found Serp's body in a thicket in Ness Woods today. A clear-cut suicide, they're saying. God rest his twisted soul.

Daithi Kernanny met me on Main Street this morning and very publicly stopped to shake my hand. Typically, he'd heard a couple of the rumours about Ailis and myself but knew rightly nothing was amiss because, quote unquote, 'You're too fucking scared of me, Shay – and with good fucking reason.' Daithi appreciates a good sting and is delighted we put paid to the bypass for good. Both his brothers have pubs in the town, as you know, and depend heavily on passing trade. Oh, and not to mention the fact his wife is going to be mayor.

As a very wise man once said, all politics is local.

Shay

To: Parochial House
Dunavady

Dear Fr Noel

Humblest apologies, but I dearly needed your (very justifiable) indignation if the plan was going to work. Please find attached a bottle of the finest stuff Bushmills has ever created. I'll be issuing a statement to the *Standard* tomorrow, clarifying my position on school boundaries. It will be a complete about-turn – and I'll be paying full tribute to you for steering me back onto the path of righteousness. Of course schools have the right to define their catchment areas – if for no other reason than to curtail rush hour traffic and protect the ozone layer.

I need to ask you another favour, by the way. I'll give you a bell about it in the morning – and might call up tomorrow night to see you after the polls close.

Yours
Shay

PS Save us a drop of the aqua vitae if you could. It'll be a long time before I'm able to afford a bottle this good for myself.

McDarry Construction Ltd
Barkley Industrial Estate South
Dunavady

Dear Mr Gallagher

Work on 'The Bearpit' is completed and you can collect the keys anytime. Our decorating team finished three days ahead of schedule and very much look forward to the bonus as agreed with yourself.

I'm afraid I made the cardinal error of inviting my wife and teenage daughter around to give your place the final seal of approval. As a result, I will now be building a new master bedroom, granny flat and media room onto my own home. You only think you make money in this game.

Best of luck with the election – I'm sure you'll not disgrace us.

Yours
Darragh McDarry
MD, McDarry Construction Ltd

From: sue.mcewan@carsonville.ni
To: shay.gallagher@freedunavady.com

Oh, all right, I'll call up tonight for an hour. Seeing as how you're going to need somebody's hand to hold when Dexter Hart whips that fine arse of yours.

And yes, I'll bring Dani. But Gran wants to come up for the count as well. Crazy lady thinks you invited her. Say it ain't so, Shay.

Seriously, pet, it's been more than a month, and a girl has needs – even us good Protestant girls. My hands are starting to shake – and not in a good way.

Love you
Sue

From: shay.gallagher@freedunavady.com
To: rosannas.flowers@freedunavady.com

Come on, Rosie

I can't do this without orchids. Give your pal in Derry a ring – and don't worry about the few extra bob. (I hear you're minted.)

Shay

From: thomas.mginlay@freedunavady.com
To: shay.gallagher@freedunavady.com

Shay

Well done, ye fine thing, ye. I've just seen the first exit polls and you're going to win by 4,000. Dex's tally is up slightly because of all the good publicity he's got over the last week, but Fulcroom's vote is evaporating quicker than the steam off my irritable bowel movements. (I do hope you're eating.)

I'll stay at the count centre until it's all over – probably about midnight – then meet you at Fr G's. I invited Ed O'Conway, Chris Caddle and Barney Deverry as well. And Stan Stevenson, of course. Boy, is he keen to scrub that egg off his face.

Oh, and I sorted out that other matter with two phone calls. I don't know who the hell was talking to Sue – but they'd got it all arse-about-face.

Tommy B

PS I've been trying your mobile all day – but you're quite right to keep it off until you've got the all clear. And you know me, I can't work this txting stuff.

From: dani@carsonville.ni
To: shay.gallagher@freedunavady.com

Hi, Shay

Trust this will reach you on your I-Phone. Mum's in the car on the way up – I'll be there with Gran at ten.

I think she's twigged. Strike that – I know she's twigged. The idiot caterer couldn't get you, so he rang her and asked how many bottles of champagne for the reception. I tried to pretend it was a civic function in your honour after the count, but Mum's quick as a three-card trick. She rang Rosanna's Flowers and asked if they'd any orchids, only to be told there were none left – there'd been a terrible rush on them this morning.

Anyhow, I don't think she's too despondent – she spent the rest of the afternoon in the hairdressers, then went into Omagh and splashed out £1,500 on a new Gerry Weber outfit.

Just don't blow your lines now, you big Jessie.

Oh, and by the way, Tommy just rang about the adoption. Seems you're going to be stuck with me as well.

I suppose I really should thank you.

Your loving daughter
Danielle Gallagher

PS And, Shay, thanks. Really.

EPILOGUE

Par Avion
To: Shay Gallagher, Member of Parliament
Hotel St Christopher
Basseterre
St Kitts

Dear Shay

Enclosed is the latest edition of the *Standard*, as promised. Hope the holiday is going well and that you're not neglecting your suntans. The smart money is saying you'll both come back whiter than when you left. And it'll be nothing to do with Sue's fair skin either.

Things are getting back to normal here after the high drama of recent weeks. I've checked in on Dani and Gran, and they seem to be adjusting well to the new house – as much as I could tell, at least. They barely looked round from the 60-inch High Definition TV. Talk about a realistic picture – if I'd had one of those babies and a Swedish satellite, I'd never have needed to get married.

By the way, election night was magic – what a party! The police tried to close down the parochial hall shortly after you left for the airport, but Ed O'Conway overruled them on the grounds that Fr Giddens hadn't opened his special reserve yet, the tight old git. Ed sends his regards, by the way – and is demanding a tour of the Commons as soon as you get back.

Jack White, as you'd expect, never dropped his guard for a minute, even with a good quarter-gallon of whiskey in him. True to form, he waited until everyone had confessed all their dirty little secrets before cowping over in the cloakroom. (Happily for all our sakes, I managed to get a bagful of incriminating photographs of him!) Your speech was a killer, I must say. I quoted a chunk from it in the article, as you'll find – though, naturally, I tidied up your grammar and cut out all the boring bits.

Seriously, though, you did a marvellous job – both with the campaign and with all that went before. Anyway, enjoy your time with Sue, and come back to us all safely.

I'm very proud of you, Shay.

Stan

GALLAGHER SCORES DOUBLE TRIUMPH

North Derry MLA Shay Gallagher confounded the experts on Thursday night, not by winning the vacant Westminster seat but rather by surrendering his much-cherished bachelorhood at a private ceremony immediately after the count. After defeating his closest rival Dexter Hart by capturing 54 per cent of the poll, Gallagher stunned the crowd when he ended his acceptance speech by asking his long-term fiancée Susan McEwan if she would marry him that night.

And there were loud whoops of both delight and relief (mostly the new MP's), when, after a nail-biting, thirty-second-long pause, the new Mrs Gallagher consented.

"It was the least I could do," she grinned. "He's kept me waiting for five years."

Mr Gallagher, who is the youngest MP ever to represent the borough, joked that his new alignment was "pretty conventional", given some of the arrangements that have emerged over the past couple of years. "Though, unlike our current First and Deputy First Ministers," he said, "I can confirm that my new partner and I will hold hands in public."

Gallagher survived a media onslaught on his campaign when both he and Dexter Hart were accused, wrongly, of accepting improper payments. Both men have since been commended for their role in an undercover operation to catch racketeers.

Mr Gallagher alluded to the sting during his victory address, saying: "It does no harm for politicians to break out of the mould occasionally and actually work in the interests of the wider public. I know this seems to run counter to how we're expected to act. But, incredible as it may seem, it is sometimes possible to use our Machiavellian instincts for the common good."

'Saint Shay'

In his concession speech, Dexter Hart paid tribute to his opponent before commiserating with the new Mrs Gallagher. "Saints are hard to live with," he quipped, "not that you'll have to put up with that for too long, given that fella's pedigree."

On a serious note, he added that he, Gallagher and the former Miss McEwan would be aligning at Stormont (yes, another new alignment) to introduce robust legislation on lobby reform.

"We're running our own government a wet week, and there are already guys pulling more strokes up here than Fianna Fáil did down South in eighty years," he said.

"If anything, we're learning far too quickly. We have to tackle the issue of graft first day. There is no point in spending the rest of our lives bogged down in tribunals. The wealthy must be stopped from buying, or blackmailing, their way to political power. We cannot replace one generation of faceless men with another, even if there are now a few Catholics in their ranks."

Best man

As soon as the speeches were finished, the throng headed to St Fiachra's Parochial Hall where Monsignor Noel Giddens and Canon Metcalfe Johnson were ready to concelebrate the wedding.

Thomas McGinlay, Mr Gallagher's agent, swapped his traditional bow tie for a white cravat to act as best man; Dexter Hart was groomsman; and Stanley Stevenson served as chief usher. Danielle McEwan-Gallagher was chief bridesmaid; Lindsay Kilturk, Ms McEwan's PA, also attended her, while Siofra

CONTINUED...

Kernanny was flower girl.

The happy couple left the following morning for the Caribbean. They were, of course, driven to the airport.

The party at the Parochial Hall continued until well into Friday evening, when the last of the stragglers were finally thrown out to allow the Dunavady Bridge Club to set up their tables.

There were no arrests.

Praise for Garbhan Downey

RUNNING MATES (2007)

Irish News: Irresistibly funny. A wickedly sharp and often hilarious portrayal of the ubiquitous crookery that takes place behind closed doors in the run up to an election.

Irish Independent: Downey's latest offering is unashamedly creating a new kind of genre – the Irish cross-border political thriller... Its rapid-fire pace, intriguing twists, high body count, and brilliant dialogue make it a really exciting read, and a worthy addition to the ever-growing list of classy Irish crime novels.

Sunday Business Post: Fast-paced, outlandish and funny.

Irish Mail on Sunday: This blackly humorous romp fizzes with dark wit and has a razor sharp edge.

Kenny's Books, Ireland (Fiction Book of the Month, July 2007): A roller-coaster tale – a good cynical look at the Northern attitude towards the South and vice versa.

New York Irish Voice: He's a bit of one, is Garbhan Downey. In his new novel, a fast-paced satire of Irish politics and political life, thinly veiled Irish public figures are given the full treatment... It just so happens that Downey has a talent for writing vivid dialogue in the Irish vernacular that makes this outrageous caper work on its own terms.

News Letter: A really good book . . . a brilliantly plotted and written comedy romp through a tremendously corrupt race for the Irish presidency.

Ulster Herald: His style captures the fly-boy humour and wise-cracking lack of deference of his Derry city home. Yet it is his knowledge of what former Irish President Erskine Childers once described longingly as the "cut and thrust" of Irish party politics that gives *Running Mates* its surprising authenticity. This work of fiction will amuse and inform anybody with even an inkling of interest in Irish politics in a new era. This is one to savour.

Alternative Ulster: Fictional gold . . . a hilarious romp through affairs of state.

County Times: The plot, which is ingeniously constructed, has the fingerprints of a master craftsman and propels Downey to the forefront of the fictional writers of the day. If it is your intention to buy only one book this year, then let it be this.

OFF BROADWAY (2005)

Sunday World: A belly-laugh-on-every-page collection of short stories which will shoot to the top of the shoplifters' book-of-the-week almost overnight . . . Garbhan must have got the gen on every racket and scam in the city.

Modern Woman: A master stylist . . . Dammit, you can almost taste the steam off the pages.

Ireland on Sunday: Nothing is sacred . . . many laugh-out-loud moments.

Daily Ireland: A nail-biting read. It's sharp, cynical, often caustic, but always enjoyable.

Woman's Way: A viciously funny look at the rise of crookery and roguery in Ireland since the ceasefires.

Derry Journal: An instant hit . . . From the smoking gun to the smoking suitcase, *Off Broadway* gives the genteel reader an insight into what is really going on all over the post-ceasefire North. I have already sent a copy hotfoot to Michael McDowell, the Republic's Minister for Justice.

Books Ireland: If you can't see what's funny about Ulster politics, take a dose.

PRIVATE DIARY OF A SUSPENDED MLA (2004)

Sunday Times: The best Northern Ireland political novel of the century.

Irish News: If there is anything good that came out of the suspension of the Assembly, it has to be the idea which inspired Garbhan Downey to write *Private Diary of a Suspended MLA*.

Sunday Tribune: A hilarious romp.

Belfast Telegraph: A gem . . . this new author is eagle-eyed and as sharp as a lance.

Hot Press: Rude'n'racy . . . gleefully sends up the Northern political process.

Eamonn McCann, Sunday Journal: By the time I had read the second paragraph I knew it was going to be a tour de force.

Derry News: Expect a literary smack in the mouth.